Discovering Me

Discovering Me

Intempus

Divyanjali Verma

PARTRIDGE

To order additional copies of this book, contact
Partridge India
000 800 10062 62
orders.india@partridgepublishing.com

www.partridgepublishing.com/india

Contents

For Dada.

Acknowledgements

Thank you,

Divyansh Verma, for showing me the beautiful sky

Isophia, for giving me the wings to fly

Aditi Sharma, for being the wind under my wings

For without you I would never have had flown.

Thanks to my family and my friends for making me believe in myself. To all the people at Partridge Publishing who were most helpful throughout the publishing process. Lastly, I extend my warmest thanks to Shatakshi Agarwal, who was always there to bounce ideas off, to ask questions which modified and shaped what I had written and also for being one of my muses. Without whom, the story would not have been more than a mere chapter long.

Thank you.

-Divyanjali Verma.

Warning

Dear Reader,

This story was supposed to be a one-shot which then grew into a book, which in turn, because of its length and many cliffhangers (Sorry but there will be a lot of those. Don't say I didn't warn you!) had to be broken down into a series.

All this simply means that there might be some places where you think that I have clearly not done any research but fear not, all of it has an explanation, if not in this book then the next, or perhaps in the one after that.

So here I am, warning you, to pay attention to the smallest of details because almost every random sentence is significant.

Have fun reading!

-DV

Prologue

"Drive! Now!" Melissa shouted as she got into the car, throwing the grocery bags in the back. Laurent just pressed the accelerator in reply. He was an exceptional driver, weaving his way through the moving traffic quite easily but the words from his fellow passenger were making him anxious. Melissa, who was looking back through the rear windshield at the car tailing them, kept saying things like- "We've lost them." "Oh no! They've caught up again." And most of all, "Laurent!"

Knowing that the other was in danger was their trigger and at that moment, when both their lives were in danger, letting go was not an option. Laurent shifted into a faster lane.

The two had known each other for almost the entirety of their lives, rendering the features of the other as familiar to them as their own. Melissa with her raven colored hair, and steel grey eyes, and Laurent with his sandy blond hair and similarly colored eyes. He loved her smile, the real one, which spread her cupid's brow beautifully, and made laugh lines appear at the corner of her eyes. For her part, Melissa too tried her best to make him laugh. It brought to view the dimple on his left cheek, about which he was so self-conscious, for a split second before he hid it by schooling his expression into one which conveyed annoyance instead of mirth. At that moment though, neither of them smiled.

"Mel. Act your age and shut up!" Laurent growled, forcing her to buckle up as he changed gears and increased the car's speed again, driving just under the limit. The fact that it was not even dawn yet, worked in their favor as the roads were empty which reduced the risk of collision to nil.

Suddenly, a grey SUV came in front of them and he stomped on the breaks, avoiding contact but dangerously swerving the car. The two of them could do nothing but watch as six figures dressed all in black got out of the vehicle. Melissa felt Laurent grab her hand and she squeezed it in reply, knowing that being so outnumbered, and powerless, their being on the run for twenty seven years, three months, one week and two days was finally coming to an end.

"We're finally going to meet them," she whispered. He nodded in silence and leaned forward to kiss her goodbye. Their napes glowed with a golden light, two symbols in sharp relief against the brightness on each, just as fire engulfed their car and it burnt with them inside, watched silently by the cloaked people.

One of the onlookers then reached into a hidden pocket from their jacket and took out a phone. Calling the only number on it, he spoke just two words. "It's done."

The Past

She stood, with her hands on the cast iron railing of the bridge, gazing down at the swirling grey waters of the Snohomish River which reflected the stormy sky above. The wind that blew ruffled the skirt of her dark blue dress around her knees as well as her hair around her face. The coolness of the metal which flowed into her palms, steadily seeped away the warmth, as if trying to help her concentrate on something other than her thoughts. It failed in its task though, because the color of the water reminded her over and over again of the encounter which she had had just a while earlier with a person having eyes of the same hue.

She was not one to dwell much on her past. She had always believed in living the present and being ready for the future. Maybe this very tendency was what had forced the very worst of her personal demons to catch up on her so suddenly that she could no longer run away from it. It had caught her, held her tightly in its clutches, refusing to let go, and the decision which weighed her down at the moment was too much to take.

Danielle Hayes was barely twenty seven years old, her birthday having occurred a week before, on the fourth of September. Her appearance was uncommon, with her waist length hair, so dark brown that they looked almost black, flowing down her back in a cascade of pin-straight strands, her eyes, a rare bluish-grey, an aristocratic nose and high cheekbones on a slightly oval face. She was of a petite height of five feet three inches, which normally did not attract much respect and seriousness, but she held herself as if she were the Queen of the world. On seeing her from afar, some called her proud, some called her arrogant, but there were some who had no word for her other than beautiful.

In spite of her high qualifications, she worked as a teacher in an elementary school, a very stable job with bright and smiling faces all around her; something that was interchangeable with a 'happy' atmosphere. Of course, this was in obvious contrast to all that she had left behind and now, as her past and present had collided so painfully, all she could do was take a day off to think of her next step. She shut her eyelids as the wind whipped her hair around her face, blowing a strand into her eyes. She reached up to brush it away and then, taking a deep breath, opened them again. A drop of water fell on her nose and she sniffed in surprise. That apparently was the signal for the heavens to open up as a light drizzle began falling around her almost immediately. She sighed, turning away from the railing, and began making her way to her apartment, two blocks away.

As she walked on the glistening concrete with the tiny droplets chilling her slightly, she meditated on the memories of all that had led up to that lightbulb moment which had just occurred an hour before.

* * * * *

At the age of five, when she had started her schooling, Danielle had often been teased about the fact that she did not look like her parents and also that she did not have the same surname as them. She did ask frequently at home why she was not a blond like her younger sibling or why she did not have emerald eyes like her parents. It was not until seven years later, at the age of twelve that she discovered the truth.

She still remembered the moment that the dam of lies had broken and the reality was revealed, as clear as day. Danielle had just come back from the park after having played the whole evening away with her friend, Myra Mills, and was red-faced from all the running that she had done. She was recounting her day to her mother as they walked through the main door and stopped mid-laugh as they noticed her father staggering his way through the doorway from the kitchen. "David?" Danielle's mother cried along with her daughter's worried, "Daddy!"

David flinched at their loud voices and with a menacing look on his face, turned his gaze onto Danielle and growled, "Don't call me 'Daddy'. I'm not your father." And he took another swig from the whiskey glass in his hand, the fluid's dark shade displaying its strength.

Danielle looked dazed as she turned to face her mother. "Mu-?" She began to ask but stopped when she saw her mother's face as she looked at David with a horrified expression on her face and said, "No David…" well, pleaded actually.

"What?" He asked angrily. "We both know that it's true, that you found her in that orphanage near your office and pestered me into agreeing to adopt her. I didn't want her but it was you who were hell bent on keeping her in spite of what I said. Not me. You, Rebecca, only you! And now we're stuck with her!"

"Baby-" Rebecca started, but Danielle cut her off with a cold, "I don't care what you have to say, it will be just another of the millions of lies you must have been feeding me all these years. So for both of our sakes, don't bother looking for me."

With that she spun around and left. The last images of her so-called parents, Rebecca, on her knees, sobbing, and David, smiling contentedly with the whiskey glass still in his hand, imprinted in her mind. But it was not until she was about a block away that the tears started to pour unstoppably, in spite of all her efforts.

* * * * *

As Danielle reached her apartment, she fished out the keys from her bag, opened the door and wandering into the kitchen, took out a bottle of cool water from the refrigerator.

Resting against the counter, she forced herself to remember again. *'Perhaps there might've been something that I missed.'*

* * * * *

Danielle had ridden a bus to a nearby town where no one knew who she was and paid for the ride with the only money that she had in her dress' pocket. Seeing her there alone, the local police department tried to make her tell where she lived. However, Danielle refused to speak and since her adoptive parents had not filed a 'missing' report, she was put under foster care.

Six years and too many to be true foster homes later, when she was finally a legal adult, Danielle ran away one last time to Seattle, where, by working at a café, she supported her living arrangements and a BA in English and Economics at Seattle University. Even with moving around so much in foster homes, she was a bright student and had thus managed to land a scholarship which took care of most of her fees. Then she went on to do her Masters, ending up as the top of her year. After finishing her education, instead of agreeing to a great job offer with a comfortable pay, Danielle moved to Snohomish, a small town northwest of Seattle, and started working at an elementary school, teaching around thirty students the basics of the language, year after year. Her future goals extended only till her lesson plans.

* * * * *

'Until now.' Danielle thought with an inward groan, as she replaced the newly refilled bottle into the refrigerator and sitting on one of the high stools in her kitchen, took out the letter from her handbag. Fingering the unopened envelope she thought back on how it had reached her in the first place.

* * * * *

The day had started off as usual, with her going to the school after breakfast, spending the whole morning with the children and then after having lunch at home, going to a book café nearby where she bought a cold coffee and settled into her favorite chair in the back, after picking out a battered copy of 'Little Women', one of her favorite books, which no matter how old she was, she always loved reading.

She had just gotten to the part where Jo first meets Laurie, when she noticed a shadow falling upon her. Raising her head, she looked up at a young man in his twenties standing in front of her with a peculiar expression on his face, one which she could not decipher. He was moderately tall, reaching almost six feet, and wore black jeans, paired with a grey shirt. His features looked familiar, ruffled dark brown hair, high cheekbones, a sharp nose and a proud chin. However, Danielle could have sworn that she did not know him.

"Excuse me, I'm sorry, but are you...are you Danielle Hayes?"

Danielle frowned. There were not many strangers who came to town especially not strangers looking for her. "Yes, I am. Who's asking?" she replied, her voice a bit colder than it usually was, because, for some strange reason, she had a really bad feeling about him.

However, nothing could have prepared her for his reply, and Danielle felt as if she was hit by a truck when she heard him speak. "I'm Daniel Hayes, your brother."

Danielle stared at him for one long moment and then suddenly, got up and did the only thing she had always done in situations like this. She ran. Out of the café, into the street, book and coffee forgotten, muttering "No. No. No." all the while. She could not believe that this was happening after all these years, when she had finally managed to accept the possibility that she would never have a real family to speak of. It was as if someone did not want her forgetting, did not want her to let go. That was exactly what she did not want and hence she surged, painfully aware of the throbbing in her feet as she surged on the hard concrete in her dainty sandals. Danielle could hear his shoes hitting the ground, sounding closer with every step she took. However, even as she moved, she could not shake off the fact that he did bear resemblance to her.

She felt a hand on her shoulder and jerking it off, she turned around, not bothering to wipe the tears that ran down her cheeks.

"No! Leave me alone. I don't need you. Not now."

"But I do!" Daniel urged, his hands holding both of hers now. She shot her head up at this, and looking into her eyes, he said softly, "I do, Danielle."

"But why? Why now? Why come for me *after* I stopped hoping that you people would find me? Just...why?

"Can we sit somewhere? Because the story's a bit long." Daniel said. Taking a minute to calm herself, she nodded and led him towards a nearby park where they sat on adjacent swings. Lightly swinging, while Danielle sat absolutely still, Daniel started speaking. "Let me start from the beginning. I'm Daniel Hayes, son of Laurent and Melissa Hayes and I'm twenty two years old. Also, I didn't know that you existed till three days ago."

"How...?" Danielle began.

"How did I finally find about you?" Daniel finished and Danielle nodded.

"Through our parents' will. They died four days back." He said quietly.

Danielle felt the sharp stab of sorrow as she heard the news and then she hung her head, accepting the inevitable fact that she would never get to meet her birth parents.

* * * * *

"Ever wonder why your name is 'Danielle *Hayes*'?" He asked after a while.

Danielle nodded in reply, thinking back to all the times in her childhood when she had pondered over that very fact, wondering where this was going.

"Well, when mom left you on that orphanage's door, she left just one thing with you, besides your blanket. It was a letter, a letter begging whoever take care of you to name you as such and before you ask me how I know this, it was in a missive she wrote to me which I received three days ago, the one that told me of your existence."

Daniel was silent for a while and then continued, "You have a home, you know? You could come live with us."

"Us?"

"Yeah, our grandma and I, we live together. You could come, it's pretty lonely anyways and you wouldn't even have to work! We have plenty of money to support us for centuries to come."

"What?" Danielle was shocked. How did he think that she would just go along with whatever he said when they met just a few minutes ago?

Daniel raised his hands as if in surrender and said, "I'm not asking you to pack your stuff and leave right now. I was merely suggesting it. Even if you don't want to come live with us, you could at least visit. Grandma would be ecstatic to see you."

Danielle released the breath which she had not even realized she was holding and mumbled, "Yeah maybe."

He stood up then and brushing dust off the back of his jeans, took out a sealed envelope from his pocket and gave it to Danielle.

"This was written by mom to you. You might want to read it, as I'm sure it would answer some of your questions and if there's still something you want to know, call me." And he handed her a slip of paper with his name and number written on it.

Then, he turned to leave, but hesitating at the last moment, pivoted and leaning down, placed a soft kiss on her cheek. "I really hope that you make the right choice and maybe come along with me."

He left then, leaving behind a shocked Danielle, her hand rising to touch where he had kissed her.

* * * * *

Looking at her name written in beautiful swirling script on top of the yellowed-with-age envelope once again, Danielle broke the strange looking seal and took it out. Glancing at the ceiling one last time as she sighed again, she opened the letter which could either provide closure or open fresh wounds.

Dear Danielle, (if you're named thus)

If you're reading this, it means that I am no longer alive and also that I didn't get to meet you, which I deeply regret.

I've written this one so many times but I'm still not sure as to how to tell you. It's been a long, long time for me since I last met you and so pardon me if this does not come out right. I know that you have many questions and I hope that this answers them all...

I had you when your father and I were nineteen and even if we were married, we were deemed too young to have a child of our own and were forced to give you up. I sincerely beg you to believe me when I say that I love you and never wanted to let go of you. That's the reason why I named your brother after you. I don't know if the people who brought you up complied with my request to name you what I had, Danielle Hayes, a name I adored and loved with all my heart just as I loved you.

I know that you must be wondering why I didn't come to find you. Well, that was the result of my being a coward. Yes, a coward. I was scared that you'd reject me and that was what kept me from searching for you, even though I wanted to so much and I am sorry for that.

There is so much to talk about right now but I cannot find words to express myself. Even if I am gone, I hope that Laurent is the one delivering this to you and if he's not... Oh baby, I'm so sorry!

I wish that I never send this...

Love you with all my heart,

Melissa.

It was not until she saw some ink dissolving in droplets of clear liquid that Danielle realized that she was crying and when she did, it did not take long for her to break down in sobs, clutching the letter, the only evidence of her mother's love, to her heart.

People say that crying soothes us but in that moment, it only led to a heart wrenching pain that had her crying into her hands, the tears running through the gaps in her fingers and falling on the already blotchy piece of paper now lying on the kitchen slab.

When she finally ceased crying, after what felt like hours, she raised her head, wiped away her tears, got up, washed her face at the sink, picked her bag, rummaged through it and finally pulled out her phone and a paper which read 'Daniel Hayes' and dialed the number on it. The call was picked up after three rings.

"Daniel? Yeah, it's me. Is the offer still open? I want to go home."

Blood

Five minutes after Danielle had hung up the phone, she could have hit herself for her impulsive reaction. How could she be so…so gullible as to think that whatever a stranger had told her was true? She did not even know her real parents' names! So how could she just believe? Believe that the letter, which could have been written by anyone, came from her birth mother! She had mourned strangers when 'Daniel' had told her about 'their' parents. Was she truly so desperate for the idea of 'family'? So easily believing someone who could very well have been a stalker or a kidnapper, who had dug up information about her to lure her away! Well, he was barking up the wrong tree if that was the case. There was no one to offer ransom for her or anything like that, so it made no difference as to what happened to her. But using her parents? That was hardly a way to entice her! Or maybe not so stupid after all, because she had fallen for the lie, hadn't she? She had fallen for it hook, line and sinker.

'What in the world is wrong with you?' She berated herself over and over again.

Her parents, real, adoptive, and foster, were all sore point with her. Having been abandoned by the first, having left the second, and sent away from the third had left her quite sensitive on that front. So, after finishing college, she finally decided to give herself the closure she needed and had set out to find out her birth parents. She had spent almost three years looking for them, contacting adoption agencies, organizations that helped find adopted kids find their real parents, even hiring a PI when all else failed, but to no avail. It was as if they never even existed. No names, no pictures, no residential address, no workplace, nothing!

Eventually, she had simply given up, convincing herself that she never wanted to meet them anyways because who in their right mind would have left their child in an orphanage?

Over the next few years, Danielle had thought about her birth parents many times, sometimes sympathizing with them by telling herself that being unaware of under what conditions they had lived, maybe it had been the better choice to let her go, and that, given similar circumstances, she probably would have done the same. Other times, she was angry at them, not knowing who they were, because no matter what their living conditions had been, no child deserved to be left with no means of finding their way back home.

She berated herself for her momentary lapse in judgment when the bell rang and the spy-hole in the door revealed Daniel. *'If that's really his name.'* Her mind working quickly, she formulated a plan to check his credibility, even as she opened the door with a tamed expression to admit him.

"Nice place," he commented, as she watched him take in the sight of the room which could indeed have been called 'nice', in the vaguest and most polite description. The drawing room had plain white walls, unadorned with anything but a thin layer of dust which made obvious the resident's negligence of the house. There were no decorations in the room and the furniture consisted of a dark wood sofa set and a glass topped table, on which lay the morning's newspapers, as well as those which were two or three days old. That was it. Looking around, no one could have told that the flat was inhabited by a woman, or by anyone actually, let alone the fact that the occupant had been living there for almost three years.

"Thanks," Danielle muttered, not knowing that he was being sarcastic or simply being condescending but she paid no attention to it. "Can I get you anything? Tea? Coffee?" she asked.

"Oh, don't worry, plain water is just fine." Daniel replied, settling down on the sofa, when she indicated him to do so.

Danielle nodded and walked over to the kitchen, returning with a glass of water. "Thanks." he said, taking it from her and she watched in silence as he sipped on the cool liquid. "You wanted to talk?" he asked awkwardly. Danielle continued to stare at him, aware that her scrutiny was unnerving him, probably more than any glare ever had by the looks of it. Danielle smiled at his discomfort as she fixed him the best teacher-like stare that she could, one which made all the children in school listen to her. His expression changed, as if something was telling him that maybe coming over and being so was not really right somehow. Her smile widened.

"Well Dan, may I call you Dan? It's weird calling somebody else by my name." He nodded in agreement as Danielle continued. "Well Dan, since we just met, I thought that it would be better that we spent some time together. Reconciling, sharing memories and the like, you know?"

"Yeah, sure, whatever you say." Dan was quick to agree. "I'm staying in a motel nearby, I could come around whenever you call."

"That would be great!" Danielle smiled again. "And I'd love it if you spent the night here, I'm making spaghetti."

She noticed that he let himself relax at her words. Apparently he had not expected her to invite him to dinner, much less stay the night. Something seemed to tell him to keep his guard up, to bear in mind the fact that her invitation might not have been as innocent as he otherwise might have thought. However, she thought she saw him mentally shrug this thought away and putting his glass back on the table, he looked up at her, smiling. "Need any help in the kitchen?" he asked. Danielle nodded in reply and led him through to that very place.

* * * * *

The next morning, as she bade Dan goodbye for the day, Danielle could not help but smirk after he turned around to leave. She went out, locking the door behind her, to meet an acquaintance of hers, who coincidentally happened to be a forensic technician. He had always been friendly with her, overly friendly in her personal opinion, but she now figured that he would be the best man to help her out in this particularly intimate matter. Visiting him at his workplace, Danielle greeted Andrew with a smile that only the most expert psychologists could possibly have determined as fake.

She felt a slight pang of guilt for using this easy-going young man, with bright red hair, light blue eyes and a smile on his slightly round face which brightened up even the saddest day.

"I need a favor, Andrew," she replied, sweetly.

"Glad to help. What do you need me to do?" he asked, his expression serious, though his eyes were still welcoming.

Danielle told him all that she needed him to do and although it was evident that he wanted to know more, he complied with her request and offered to accompany her home so that she did not have to make a second trip unnecessarily. Danielle agreed and the two made the short journey to her apartment in his car, for she had walked over to his place.

She left Andrew waiting in the car while she went into the flat to retrieve what she needed. Danielle walked over to the couch on which Daniel had slept and feeling another smile creep up on her face, she picked up the pillow that he had used and donning the gloves that she had been given by him, carefully plucked a couple of hair which were caught in the fabric. Dropping them carefully in an accompanying sterilized evidence bag, she ran a hand through her own hair and put the strands that came off into another evidence bag. Then she walked back down where Andrew was waiting in his car and handed over both bags to him.

"I'll get back to you with the results as soon as I can," he promised. Then he drove away.

Danielle, having murmured her thanks, then turned back to enter the building with a smile on her face. A smile which was as true as the one which she had flashed Andrew just a few moments earlier had been false.

* * * * *

It was two days later, while Danielle was taking her last class before lunch break, that her phone rang. Apologizing to her students, she went out in the corridor and picked up the incoming call.

"I did the test," Andrew's voice came through the speaker of the phone. "And Danielle, he is related to you. Not sure if he is your brother or not but he is definitely related to you, there's a twenty five percent DNA match."

Danielle found herself speechless. All those years of searching and when she finally found someone, it was because they'd came to her. But wait! She had a family. Someone related to her by blood. She need not be alone in the world any longer because she, Danielle Hayes, finally had found her family!

"Danielle? You still there?" she heard Andrew speak. She had forgotten that he was still on the line.

"Yes. Thank you Andrew, thank you so much," she replied, her voice wavering slightly.

"You going to tell me what that was all about, now? Why did you need a DNA test done? Danielle? Hello? Danielle?" She pressed the end-call button, a smile on her face. A smile that remained there the whole day through, pleasantly surprising her students.

That afternoon, when she returned home, she called Dan over for lunch. While she waited for him, she made one more impulsive decision, wondering lightly whether its consequences would be like her earlier moment of spontaneity, or as she had termed it, moment of insanity. She sat down and drafted her resignation from her job, along with a two-week's notice for her landlady. She thought about Andrew and the students, but the thought of meeting and finally being with her family overwhelmed the choice of staying back. She had considered not resigning as she did not know whether she would be staying there anyway, but something compelled her to believe that she would not be returning to Snohomish anytime soon. Danielle

Elle

The lies told to her all those years ago had made Danielle extremely suspicious of others. As protection from further lies, she had closed herself off, building a mental wall around herself and then hiding behind a stoic mask at all times. She did not allow herself to feel, to get close to someone lest they hurt her. Even the apartment which she had had for three years housed just the bare necessities, very different from expectations after being occupied by a woman for so long.

Danielle had become so closed off that by now, that even if there were a million thoughts running through her mind, she could control her reactions like an actor. No one knew about her inner turmoil. She loathed changes because they upset her carefully ordered life. Thus, when Daniel had so abruptly appeared, it was taking all her inner strength to not run away again, to escape from such momentous changes.

However, she had handed her two-week' notices to both her workplace and her landlady.

She had also asked Daniel to move in with her for the fortnight as she did not like the idea of him living in a motel, or so she said. In reality, she was just trying to convince herself that all of it was actually happening. Following a bad psychological breakdown in the past, she was not always convinced of the reality around her because she knew that hallucinations were not all that different. So, even though the DNA results locked up in her safe reported otherwise, she had her misgivings that Dan could simply be a product of her imagination. It was no surprise then that she was a wreck internally, an ongoing war within her about whether her comfortable, if lonely, life at Snohomish was worth leaving or not. Thankfully Daniel had not declined and did stay at her apartment, finally making her accept that it was real, that it was actually happening.

When the day to leave finally arrived, Danielle sent her brother down to keep her sole suitcase in his car while she went to hand over the keys to her landlady, Mrs. Blake, a woman in her sixties, had tears in her eyes as she pulled Danielle into a hug. Danielle had felt herself pulling away automatically. As she descended the steps from the third floor, she wondered what could have made Mrs. Blake sad to see her go, when, if she was in her place, Danielle would surely have been happy to see a tenant, who did not even speak except for when handing over the rent, leave.

Bidding farewell to Mrs. Blake reminded her of her students and Andrew once again, but moving past the slight pang of guilt that she felt, Danielle followed Dan.

* * * * *

He looked up to see Danielle exiting the building and with a light caress to the side of the car, got into the sleek Mercedes convertible. She stood there on the driveway for a moment or two before Dan revved up the engine, grinning at the haste with which she climbed in.

"Hey Dan?" Danielle asked as they backed off onto the road.

"Hmm?"

"Since it's going to be a long ride, wake me up when we get there? I didn't sleep too well last night." Danielle requested.

"All right, I will." Dan replied nonchalantly, hiding the fact that in reality he was a little disappointed. He had been looking forward to talk some more with his sister, because in the past fortnight their conversations had barely exceeded the topics of food and weather and he had hoped that being in the confines of a car would perhaps open her a bit more. *'And maybe I'll find out why she was so happy to see me leave if she had been planning on coming along after all.'*

He had been better acquainted that fortnight about how mistrusting she generally was. Even asking him their destination had been filled with underlying skepticism.

"Could I call you 'Elle' I mean, the same logic that you used to call me 'Dan' can be used here too. It's weird calling somebody else by your own name!"

"That's alright." Danielle replied as she spooned up a small portion of the fried rice they were having for dinner.

The silence filled with the sounds of cutlery against crockery was broken by, "You never did tell me where you lived."

"Hmm?" Dan answered. "Yeah I guess so. Well, it's in Forks, so just a few hours' drive."

"Forks, Washington?"

"I didn't know that there were any others nearby." Dan joked before nodding in reply.

"Well that's good for me, I went there for a school trip a couple of years ago so I know my way around. Just don't tell me that you're a vampire though." She replied with a smirk.

He knew that his surprise was not hidden because he actually choked on his food at her light spirits and after gulping down some water, replied without much thought, "Nah. But there are some similarities." regretting the words the moment they were out.

Elle apparently noticed his voice breaking over the last word and she shut down yet again, devoting all her attention to the food. 'Way to go idiot.' Dan picked up his glass as the coughing fit subsided.

* * * * *

Meanwhile, Elle hummed a lullaby that was drowned by the car's own sound as it sped on the asphalt. The lullaby was one that she remembered, the feeling, not the person singing it, and she hummed it in a bid to fall asleep, not wanting to be awake to give incentive to her over thinking mind to once again list the pros and cons of leaving with Dan, and she willingly succumbed to the welcoming arms of sleep when it finally came for her.

Grandma

Elle woke up, feeling strange, as if warm rain had drizzled onto her but inspection revealed that she was quite dry. Chalking it up to a dream or something, Elle turned her attention to the road. She took in the familiar green surroundings that were synonymous with Forks, and looked over at Dan who was singing along softly to the stereo. He felt her watching and answered her unasked question.

"Just a few minutes more and we'll be there Elle."

Danielle nodded and looked out of the window, trying hard to remember when somebody had given her a nickname that was simply a shortening of her name, and not one to deliberately humiliate or insult her. She could not come up with anything except a faint memory of being called Ellie, but that could also be wishful thinking, for trying to recall it was like pulling something out that had been drowned way too many times to come up to the surface now. The area they were passing through looked nothing like what she remembered. She blamed the changes on time and let it pass even though there was a nagging thought at the back of her mind saying that all was not what it seemed.

As they drove deeper and deeper into the forest, she could see a double storied mansion emerging from between the green branches. It lay nestled really deep in the woods, so even though there was a road leading to it she could understand how she may have missed it the last time.

Dan drove through the huge wrought iron gates, which bore the design of intertwined vines, and stopped in front of the main doors. But 'doors' did not seem to aptly describe the magnificent structures. They were made of dark Indian Rosewood and were extensively carved with exquisite figurines, showcasing battle scenes and coronations, but the most prominent was the ethereal figure of a lady who wore a crown of vines with flowers braided in her hair. Elle wondered how long it must have taken to create the doors. The rest of the mansion was also awe-inspiring, with an impressive façade and the many balconies and walls which were draped with flowering creepers, which made it look ancient but welcoming. Daniel had not been joking when he said that the Hayes' had enough to last them for centuries.

Elle shook out of her amazement at the beauty in front of her and went to help Dan with the bags. He shook his head and instead, signaled to her to knock on the doors.

The griffin head knocker was quite loud and moments later, hurried steps were heard from inside the building. The imposing doors opened to reveal a petite, blond woman in her early thirties, whose blue eyes were warm and her smiling mouth complemented her sharp featured oval face. There seemed to be a trustworthy air about her which made Elle a bit more comfortable than she normally was, and this unsettled her.

"Hey kid, you're back early!" She grinned at Dan.

He placed the bags on the marble floor and wrapped the woman in a hug, "Of course Lynni! Didn't I say that I won't be long gone?"

'Lynni' stood on her toes to ruffle his hair affectionately and then turning to Elle, said, "And whom do I have the pleasure of meeting?"

Elle rearranged her expression into what she hoped was a smile and not a grimace, stepped forward, and offering her hand professionally, said, "Danielle Hayes, Dan's sister."

"Glad to meet you, but we don't shake hands around here," and 'Lynni' hugged a very shocked Elle who couldn't comprehend the fact that a complete stranger was hugging her, and patted Lynni's back awkwardly.

Lynni laughed, a tinkling sound that enthralled Elle, and told Dan, "Well she's just like Noah!"

Danielle thought she caught a gruffly murmured, "Don't I know it."

"Don't worry." Lynni told Dan, flashing Elle a smile.

Elle had backed away, unused to hearing people discussing her so freely.

Sensing her discomfort, the older woman smiled softly and turning to Dan she said, "Show her to her room kid and then give her a tour of the place if she wishes, I'm going to get some groceries for dinner."

Dan mumbled a response which Elle could not catch, and then picking up the bags, headed inside with Elle following him, as Lynni stepped out onto the driveway.

* * * * *

Elle's breath caught as she took in the interiors of the mansion. Entering the doorway, they had ended up in what seemed to be a long corridor that bisected the building in two. There was only one door to the left, while on the right hand side there were arched doorways, leading to rooms and other corridors presumably. At the end was a spiraling staircase that led upstairs. Dan flashed her a smile, "Let's get these to you room." He lifted her luggage in indication. She nodded in response and trailed behind him, marveling at the aged wallpaper, and peeping into the aesthetically appealing rooms as she caught their glimpse.

The siblings went to the room on the first floor beside the stairs, that had been prepared for Elle, and she was struck by how well suited to her it seemed to be.

It was a large room, with a glass wall to the right which overlooked the back garden. There was a four poster bed near the door, aligned with the glass wall, providing a perfect view of the sky when one lay down with the curtains pulled back. Elle could imagine spending nights gazing up at the stars like she always did and this made her smile. The wall opposite to the door was adorned with a floor to ceiling bookshelf of a light colored wood, with a large, black, soft-looking rug in front of it. The last wall, the one on the left, had a door, which was in line with the entry, presumably leading to the bathroom. An unusual feature was the fireplace on the last wall, over which hung a portrait of a girl holding a startling resemblance to Danielle.

Dan must have seen the confusion on Elle's face because he explained, "It was a living room before being converted into Mom's bedroom, hence the fireplace and the portrait."

"On the first floor?"

He laughed. "Who am I to say anything about our ancestors and their crazy ideas?"

Danielle was quite taken aback by the resemblance to the portrait, and for the first time since meeting Dan, and getting to know the DNA results, she finally somewhat believed that she really was going to be among family from then on. She nodded in reply and even though her expression did not change, hope and joy filled her as she considered the notion that that was actually going to be her life from then on, living with her brother in her mother's childhood home. From the corner of her eye, she noticed Dan's face breaking out into a smile. *'Maybe opening up would not be an impossible task after all.'*

* * * * *

Dan showed Elle the bathroom, which was some ways away from her room, instead of being en-suite as she had earlier thought. He explained that since the main structure of the house had not been changed during the remodeling, the lavatories were all on one side of the house. He showed her the door to Lynni's room when they passed it, after a series of other locked up bedrooms on one side and guestrooms on the other. When she entered the bath, she was not much surprised by the huge attached bathroom with a sunken marble bath in the center and a sink with toiletries beside it on a granite shelf to the side.

He then guided her back to her room, where she discovered that the other door actually lead to a dressing room and a walk-in closet. Elle ran her hands over the dresses hung in the racks. A yellow silk here, a blue taffeta there, ivy green satin and a red chiffon, hung among almost thirty other dresses and outfits, each one treasured and cared for over all the years.

Dan left Elle when she mentioned taking a bath, and picking out a deep red dressing gown from the wardrobe, she walked over to freshen up.

Pulling on a simple pair of black jeans and a purple t-shirt, she left the dressing room, and saw Dan entering the door, with a plate of waffles in his hand.

"Lynni made these. Must have guessed that we'd be hungry." He grinned as he sat on the bed. Elle joined him and they ate in a silence that was unusually tense on Dan's part.

After they finished, Dan said, "What do you want to do next Elle?" She shrugged and nodded her head at the bookshelves, "I was thinking of browsing through them."

Dan looked panicked for a second but then lightly remarked, "Oh you'll be here often enough for that. Let me show you around the house so that you don't need a guide every time you want to go somewhere."

Elle knew that the response was logical but she still could not shake off the feeling that he was hiding something from her. However, she decided not to say anything yet. So she silently got up and signaled him to lead the way.

Dan showed her his room's door, the one beside hers, 'Lynni's' room, the first floor guest rooms, the music room, study, the 'Timeless room' which held antiques and heirlooms, and another small library, before walking through another corridor. This led them to a gallery of canvasses with portraits and landscapes which ranged from beautiful women in gowns to spectacular sunrises. They were really well made and some looked like photographs rather than paintings. The interspersed windows let in natural light in a way that made the paintings glow which added to their beauty.

As they meandered on the first floor, Elle amused herself by walking along the silver vines that were embroidered on the deep blue carpets that ran in the middle of the corridors, making Dan shake his head when she tracked back after a misstep. Her fingers caressed the glass banister as they descended the marble staircase. They walked, and she felt her doubts melt away as she took in the beauty of her new home. It was a great structure which showcased the transition from medieval to modern perfectly. There were stone walls but glass doors leading to the balconies. On the ground floor, there was a ballroom with chandeliers and draperies and there was a modular kitchen too. Her most favorite room had been the impressive library which seemed to hold more books than she could ever read, but Elle was miffed at Dan since he dragged her away before she could explore. She realized with a start that he had been deliberately keeping her away from books the whole time. Elle had felt a compulsion and an impulsive need to look through them but Dan was adamant and said there were many places still to see. He showed her the guest rooms, the drawing room, the living room, the pantry, and the kitchen garden.

The last place they went was the summer house in the back beside a small pond. The staircase concealed the back door, through which there was a glass enclosed pathway leading to it through a sea of flowers. Though the summer house with its white painted wood and huge windows with a blue roof in itself was beautiful, the scene around it was even more breathtaking.

* * * * *

Dan had enjoyed showing Elle around and it was good to see the normally stoic face wonderstruck. Thus, he was not thinking much when she asked, "Didn't you say you lived with our grandmother? Where is she?"

He laughed and carelessly replied, "You already met her! Didn't Grandma Lynni open the doors for us?" And felt the temperature of the room drop.

Elle looked as if she thought that he was joking and she said, "Whatever Dan. We've had a long day and you must be tired. We'll meet her tomorrow."

He tried to respond but it was as if he had lost the ability to speak. They had reached the main corridor by then and just as Elle turned to Dan, frowning, the door opened and Lynni came in.

"Hey kid. I'm ba-" she took one look at his face and sighed, "Oh Soleus."

Dan immediately began apologizing, "Sorry Gramma, I didn't mean to..."

Lynni just shook her head as if exasperated and amused at the same time. Then she turned to a stricken-faced

Elle who was mumbling, "You're mad. Both of you..." and she started backing away.

Lynni's face grew kind and she said, "No Elle, we're not insane and neither are you. I really am your grandmother." She winked. "And well, I am actually a hundred and fifty eight year now, even though I don't look like that by human standards. I'm a Lamia dear, a witch. Dan's one too, as are you!"

Lorelei

Elle shook her head in shock and was about to run when Lynni said, "Stay." Her voice had subtly changed and Danielle found herself growing disoriented but then her head cleared.

Lynni, or Anlynne Hayes as she introduced herself to be, handed her a sealed envelope with her name on top, just like the one Dan had given her a fortnight ago, and Danielle could have sworn that it had appeared out of thin air. Anlynne looked curious to know what the envelope contained, though she kept her thoughts to herself and directed Elle into the adjacent living room. Danielle felt herself growing unreasonably and illogically calm as she walked into the room.

However, the moment she noticed this, her mind cleared. In spite of the previous suspicious haziness of thoughts, she opened the envelope and started reading the letter written in her mother's now familiar handwriting, hoping to find some answers for all the insanity.

Dear Danielle,

If you're reading this, it means that Mom gave it to you as an explanation. I know that you must be deeming us insane and also be upset with me for not telling you about this earlier, but I couldn't possibly just dump it on you in my very first letter. It would have been too Harry Potter-ish for me to write - 'Hey Danielle, know what? You're a witch.'

A small request before you cross this off. I want you to remember all the times you were exceptionally happy or sad and something strange happened. Think back to then and read on with an open mind.

Anyways, getting to the point, you're a Lamia, a witch as all of us in Peritia Imperium are.

I think that Daniel told you that you are in Forks, well technically you are but aren't too.

Ask Mom, I'm sure she'd love to tell you.

Just a few things before Mom takes over your training if you haven't already passed the age of twenty-eight. Lamias, my dear, normally have control over one or two of the three elements- air, water and fire. So the first thing to do is to identify your element/s and hone your skills to perfection. Other than that, take care to build up your physical strength too as magic cannot always be relied upon. One more thing before I finish. Don't trust anyone and everyone for everything is not always what it looks like, so be on your guard at all times.

I know that you would do amazingly well and I'm sorry again for keeping this a secret.

Much love and apologies,

Melissa.

* * * * *

It had been almost an hour since Elle had opened her mother's second letter and she had been sitting in the same place for the whole time. Dan and Lynni sat patiently, waiting for her to speak.

Even though her expression did not change, in that hour Elle had relived all the times that her mother had written about. Her room suddenly filling up with balloons on her fourth birthday. Running away a lot faster than possible when Myra had been chasing her. She also remembered her bathroom flooding when she had been crying over something her foster siblings said to her, and then the suddenly dried floor when she realized that she did not want to be humiliated by them for the freakish things that happened around her. Along with many other incidents over the years which had always scared her and it were them along with some other reasons that had led her to lock almost all her emotions away to stop these occurrences. However, all of these new developments had forced her to open up more and with this twist, she felt as if she had to do something to gain control.

Elle sighed at last and looking at Lynni, said, "Could you please explain?"

Lynni smiled and said, "It would be my pleasure dear. For a brief history- The first Lamia ever was Lorelei whose powers were given to her by Sun, or Soleus as he preferred to be called. Lorelei was twenty eight years of age when she became a Lamia, so it is that age that the Lamias gain their full strength. Anyways, Lorelei was a simple Lamia but her daughters, Paige and Yvainne, were not. They were more powerful and proficient in magic than their mother ever was and they were called the Beautiful Ones for they were ethereal in their features and no matter how many centuries passed they always looked the same."

Elle frowned at the use of the word 'centuries' and Lynni said, "Yes us Lamias are immortal if we keep away from fatal injuries or diseases. After reaching maturity our bodies age a year per half century but we will get back to that later."

Dan intervened, "All the Lamias here in Peritia Imperium, the Skill Realm, are thus Lorelei's descendants, however partly."

Anlynne chastised him, "Will you let me speak?" Dan grinned sheepishly and mimed locking his mouth and throwing away the key and Elle could not resist a small smile at their antics, then Anlynne continued.

"Contrary to what you may think the Lamias lived in the human world, well until the Witch Hunts at least. Now if we are older than twenty eight our strength wanes the longer we stay on earth so we mostly visit just for a day or two. The Hunts were a dark age for us, for Lamias were being prosecuted and their powers had been decreasing over the years with the mixing of normal human genes and thus they could not protect themselves." She paused for a moment reflective look in her eyes.

"Remember what I told you about us being immortal?" Danielle nodded. "Well Lorelei's daughters were still alive and with their powers they opened a portal to this realm and named it thus and themselves became the Guardians. It is them that we request when travelling between the two worlds."

"You may think that Peritia Imperium is very large but actually it isn't so. The Beautiful Ones, in a bid to save us, chose the area having the largest Lamian community to be safeguarded. You've seen what a fish bowl that's used for a tortoise looks like? With its base covered with gravel and water with a raised surface for the tortoise to rest on dry 'land'. Peritia is just like a giant fish bowl, containing three mountains and a valley in the center. When it was transferred to this dimension from the human one, it left a bowl shaped crater on the surface of the earth."

Anlynne let Elle ponder over the idea for a while and then continued. "At first it was a bit cramped for the Lamias but as time passed it became less congested as at the age of maturity, Lamias get to choose between their powers and humanity as more and more left it becomes easier and now there are around 10,000 Lamias in Peritia Imperium." She finished with a grim look on her face as if the dwindling numbers of the Lamias was a personal loss. 'And it kind of was.' Danielle thought.

* * * * *
_ _ _ _

Dan broke the silence which ensued, "Anything you want to ask?"

Elle took a moment to reply, "Yeah, one thing. How do we travel between the two worlds?"

Anlynne and Dan smiled and then he said, "Come I'll show you." And he got up, beckoning Elle to follow him. She looked a bit apprehensive but apparently her curiosity won and she quickly went to walk beside him.

"We have to take the car," he explained at her confused expression when he picked up his keys from the half-moon table beside the main door.

Lynni smiled encouragingly from the doorway as they got into the car.

Dan was excited to share since Elle knew the secret now but she had shut up again and was not inclined to talk. He sighed but kept quiet after a few unanswered questions. The drive was around ten minutes long but it seemed longer due to the uncomfortable silence between the siblings. Dan stopped the car and motioned for Elle to come out with him. She hesitated for a moment, perhaps because of the middle-of-nowhere look of the place, before climbing out.

"Look." Dan said, gazing at the side of the road.

She followed his gaze to a pair of ancient trees on opposite sides of the road whose canopy intermingled overhead forming an archway. Elle walked over to one of them and closer inspection of the trunk revealed a female form imprinted on the aged wood. She looked at Dan questioningly and he replied, "She is Paige, one of the Beautiful Ones."

He chuckled at her bewildered expression, the most he had ever seen on her face, and explained, "Anlynne talked about sacrificing their lives, right? Well oaks are sacred to us and so they merged themselves with the oldest trees around, forming the Gate."

Elle nodded, seemingly thinking over it and then walked through the gateway, or tried to at least. A force field prevented her from passing even a hairsbreadth through the arch.

"And how exactly do we go across it?" she asked, her annoyance, despite her composed features, clear at his amusement.

He searched his coat pockets and walking over to her handed her a paper and said, "Read that aloud and then try again."

She narrowed her eyes at him and then the paper but complied, Dan speaking along with her.

I wish to escape,

If just for some time;

While in darkness draped,

Lies my world sublime.

* * * * *

Elle felt a faint trickle of warmth, which was similar to what had awakened her up when Dan had driven them through to Peritia. She closed her eyes and took a step forward. When she opened her eyes, she was standing beside a bend in the road, instead of on the straight path that she had been a moment ago. She turned around not knowing what to expect but was not much surprised when she saw a crater shaped valley just as Anlynne had described, the view framed by the oaks of the Beautiful Ones.

When she turned around to face Dan, he smiled at her wide-with-wonder eyes. She moved her hand gingerly through the archway but was stopped by the force field again she repeated the words and tried once more but that did not work too. Dan shook his head and then said, "Turn the page around."

She did and there was another verse there and she read the words aloud, Dan doing the same from beside her.

Daughters of Lorelei,

Help me pass;

Lest I die,

By losing my powers.

This sent them back and she asked Dan with a frown on her face, "What was that all about?"

"Well since the Beautiful Ones locked us here with magic the Council decided on another layer of protection, thus the verses. The original one for entrance was longer which was later modified after complaints that saying something so long made people look insane as they would essentially be saying it to air, something which would make any human suspicious. It went-"

Daughters of Lorelei,

Help me pass;

Lest I die,

By losing my powers.

I had left,

Now I return;

Raise to the best,

My strength of the sun.

Forever grateful,

Would I be to you;

If O you Ones Beautiful,

Help us pass through.

"That is... nice." Elle commented.

Dan shrugged and opening the car door for her, said, "Shall we?"

A faint smile graced her features and she sat back in wondering if this was going to be her life now. Tales of magic, powers and different worlds and not knowing whether that would finally lead her to the happiness that she so fervently wished for.

Changing

A bloodcurdling scream tore through the silence of the night, jolting Dan from his sleep.

Anlynne had gone to spend the night with her sister, Maebel, and so he was alone, excepting the person who had screamed, Elle. In all of the fourteen nights that he had spent with her, he had listened to her walking around in her room or singing softly, not falling asleep even for a moment. She only took brief naps during the day, never at night and he was worried for her. That night was the first time that he had heard her lay down in bed in the room adjacent to his and he was glad that sleep had finally caught up to her and that she would be better rested the next day.

'If only she hadn't screamed.' Dan thought as he rushed through his door into her room where he saw her thrashing about in her sleep and shook Elle awake. She opened her eyes, frightened for a moment but relaxed as they landed on Dan. He gazed at her worriedly and she sat up, as if knowing that she would have to give an explanation sooner or later. He sensed her distress and was about to tell Elle that it was okay if she did not want to explain just then, when she sighed and looking straight into his eyes, launched into her tale.

"You want to know why I don't sleep, don't you?"

He nodded mutely, not trusting himself to speak.

"Nightmares. Nightmares keep me awake. They remind me over and over again of things that I wish to forget. Things that happened at the foster homes, at the orphanage that I was put in, things that the older kids did and said to me before they left... Whenever I sleep, all of it returns with a vengeance and I wake up screaming, clinging to the sheets, bathed in sweat, the walls ringing with the echoes of my voice and my pillows sometimes soaked in tears."

He wondered at her poetic description and watched as she looked away but continued speaking. "I've tried everything, even sleeping pills, but nothing works. Every night is the same. This is the reason that all the couples that took me in sent me back in a few months and I had to change foster homes so frequently. I'm sorry if I woke you up. I'll move back to Snohomish if you wish." Elle finished quietly, twisting her fingers in her lap, which he realized as a sign of embarrassment.

Dan got down on his knees on the rug in front of her and holding her tightly entangled hands, gently pried open each finger, and brushed his thumb against the crescents she had dug into her palms. Then, he looked at Elle's face expecting to see a change from her normally stoic expression, something to tell him what she was feeling but all he got was a blank face, no other sign of emotion other than the rapidly blinking eyelids which hid her glistening eyes, taking away a bit of their moistness with every movement.

He sighed and got up. Aware of Elle's wary eyes on him, Dan walked over to the bookshelf, pulled out a book with a dark blue cover, flipped through the pages, and finding what he was looking for, handed it over for her to read.

Elle looked at him in confusion but then proceeded to peruse what he had given her and Dan knelt in front of her on the floor again, his eyes focused on her face as she did what he had indicated. When she finally raised her head, she closed her eyes once as if deciding something and then slid down her bed to the floor in front of Dan, their knees touching. He gathered her in his arms when a lone tear slid down her face, others soon following it as she cried, her frame shaking with each sob, the tears soaking his t-shirt's front. He held her close and whispered encouraging words, not caring whether she even heard him or not because whatever her past may be did not change the fact they she was his sister and he wanted her to be happy.

Dan thought back to what he had asked her to read, as he hugged her comfortingly. It was a poem written by the famous Lamian author, Ryanelle Blackwood, titled 'Tears'.

It went-

Our eyes glisten with unshed tears,

Salty drops that show our fears;

Fear of losing someone or something,

Fear of not being able to do anything.

We try to stop them from being revealed,

Blink rapidly, to keep them concealed.

Over the years, these unshed tears,

Break our hearts and our souls they pierce.

It is better to let them flow,

Than over the years to let them grow;

For they only result in heartache,

And there's nothing to be done when their dam they break.

Don't keep your tears hidden inside,

You will feel better after you've cried;

So let them flow as they appear,

It isn't worth it to keep stopping them, my dear.

Dan rubbed her back gently as a warm fire suddenly roared to life in the fireplace, brought into existence by a wave of his hand, the glowing heat shedding light on the siblings who held each other close, afraid to let go lest the sudden need for companionship dissolve, creating a wider gap between them.

* * * * *

When Danielle woke up she felt oddly refreshed and was surprised to feel a smile on her face, something not common at all. She sat up on the rug and then turned to face Dan who lay beside her. There had been no nightmares that night and she knew that it was because of him.

'Does the 'twenty-five percent' really matter that much?' Elle hesitated for a moment and then slowly reached out to gently brush the tips of her fingers along his face. Dan's eyes fluttered open and he leaned into her hand, when she suddenly frowned. "What?" He asked.

Still in her happy daze, Elle looked searchingly into his eyes and said, "Dan, why are your eyes blue?"

He grinned at her and said, "Oh that's just a side effect of using magic. It'll return to the normal grey-blue by tonight."

Elle raised an eyebrow questioningly and he explained, "All the Lamias have a characteristic grayish-blue eye color which turns ice-blue when we use magic, it takes about a day for it to return to normal. Pretty cool though, don't you think?"

Elle nodded absently, her mind elsewhere, echoing with memories of being called 'freak' when anything remotely unnatural happened around her. She shook her head and then standing up, gave Dan a hand to help him too. After finishing up with their morning ablutions, they made their way down to the kitchen together where Anlynne was waiting for them with breakfast, having returned a while ago.

* * * * *

Polishing off the lemon waffles, Dan left for training and Anlynne invited Elle to a place she had really wanted to explore, the library.

The moment she entered the almost cathedral sized room, Elle realized that the earlier glimpse had done no justice to the magnificent store of knowledge that it was. The room was rectangular in shape and the doors were placed in the center of one of the lengths. Floor to ceiling bookshelves made of dark ebony, stood like walls in the room, their one end touching the wall opposite to the entry. Huge arched windows between the bookshelves and on either end of the chamber, let the sunbeams in to illuminate it with a golden glow. Since the outer walls of the mansion were made up of stone and were quite thick, the expanded window sills were cushioned to form seats.

The wall on which the door was situated held torches in cast iron brackets and was lined with a long table on either side to enable reading during the night.

Elle walked between the bookshelves while Anlynne watched her. She ran her fingertips over the book spines, fascinated by the heady scent of the leather, cloth or paper bound, well preserved old books. She longed to curl up in one of the window seats with one of the books and get lost in them for ages.

Something must have given away her thoughts because Anlynne called, "Danielle? You have eternity to go through each and every one of these and add a few of your own too, but right now we have work to do. We need to find a spell to break Melissa's enchantment which she placed on you to keep your powers suppressed as there is no other way that you only performed accidental magic for twenty seven years without a Mother's Spell."

Elle broke away from her trance and followed Anlynne to the left-most bookshelf, who explained, "The shelves are arranged chronologically, with the oldest on the left and the newest on the last shelf on the right. The different levels in each deal with different topics each."

With a flick of her wrist, a roll of parchment with a list of books on it appeared in Anlynne's hand. She looked through it then waved her hand gently, making a book from the top shelf float down.

Elle caught it and running a hand once on the black and gold cover, handed the book over to Anlynne who moved to the nearest window sill to sit down comfortably before opening it.

Elle sat down too and watched as her grandmother carefully leafed through the pages, finally stopping on one which had a picture of a thinning mist around a young woman's body, bearing the title- 'Rebirth'.

"What exactly are you searching for?" Elle inquired.

"Well, Mother's Spells are old magic and this is one of the oldest book on elemental magic and this spell will release your magic's bonding as nothing else will work against the Ancient Magic. Now stay still for a moment."

Anlynne put the book aside and placed the tips of her right hand's index and middle fingers on Danielle's forehead, making her jerk away in surprise. A look from the older witch led to Elle sitting stock still on the window sill and repeating her gesture, Anlynne chanted-

O Soleus, grant me the strength,

To undo the magic wreathed;

Spun in warm golden length,

As the caster lived and breathed.

Elle's breath hitched as she raised her left forearm and saw the words appearing in a ring around her wrist, as if an invisible hand was writing them in silver ink. They grew colder as Anlynne spoke and when she finished, the letters shone and then sank into her skin.

Danielle gasped at the sudden tingling warmth that filled her and looked into the startling blue eyes of her grandmother which sparked with power. She lowered her eyelids to concentrate on what she was feeling and was astounded at her discovery. It felt as if pure sunlight was flowing through her instead of blood and for a moment she was acutely aware of every part of herself and her surroundings. The ends of her hair, the chirp of the birds outside, Anlynne's heartbeat, a dust particle landing on the window pane, all was felt by her and it was infinitely beautiful. A sense of deep loss filled her as it slowly faded and she opened her eyes again to a grinning Anlynne.

"Ready to play dear?"

Hiding

Anlynne left Danielle in the library to make an appointment for a test of some kind, giving a vague description of what that entailed. Danielle learnt that there was much to be done before the actual usage of magic, one of which included these 'tests' which were simple tasks that Lamian kids undertook when enrolling in a school to check what their element was. In Peritia Imperium, the children attended morning and evening classes where in the morning they studied subjects like English, Math, Science, Latin, etc. and the evenings were devoted to Magic. Elle wanted Dan to be around while taking the tests, so Anlynne conceded to wait until his return while Elle pored over a book on magic for novices. She had been reading on a window-seat when the older witch walked in with a harried expression. In answer to Elle's questioning look she said, "Another one of your mother's letters appeared. She says that we've got to hide your identity."

"But...why?" Danielle asked her grandmother.

"I don't know. It just states that you'll be in danger if anyone knew who you really are."

Elle was about to protest when she felt a slight change in the air in front of her. She held out her hand instinctively and a piece of paper landed on it.

Just five words were written on it but they were enough to silence her protests-

'Trust me Danielle, please.

-Melissa'.

* * * * *

"Myra." Danielle spoke.

"Hmm?" Anlynne said distractedly as she read the new note.

"If I have to change my identity, I'd like to call myself Myra Mills."

Anlynne nodded and then said, "We would have to change your appearance too you know? You look way too much like Melissa." She smiled apologetically as she knew that such a change would surely not be easy, both mentally and emotionally.

Elle nodded in understanding, though still pondering over why she might be in danger and from what. After seeing the portrait in her room, she knew that a change in identity would be meaningless if her features not be changed.

"Is there a spell to do it?" Danielle asked.

Leaning against the bookshelf on the right, a thoughtful expression on her face, Anlynne replied, "Not through the normal magic as that is for controlling the elements only. No, we'll have to search for a spell similar to the one I used this morning. But, since I have no idea in which book such a spell might be found, the test may have to wait." Anlynne's still blue-with-magic-use eyes seemed sad at this but then she perked up a second later and gestured to Danielle to join her.

Elle put her book aside after noting the page number mentally and got up. Anlynne said, "It would go faster if you helped. Remember what I did for the booklist this morning? Simply concentrate on getting it before flicking and I'm sure you'll get it done. Since the book lists are magically bound to each shelf so that it self-updates when a new book is added, every list has to be collected separately from its shelf. Could you be a dear and start from the newer end? I'll bring the older ones and we'll meet back here."

Hiding her curiosity and excitement at doing magic of her own behind a cool mask, Elle shrugged and then walked past Anlynne. She walked till the end of the room, having decided to work her way towards the center.

Danielle took a deep breath to prepare herself and calm her nerves. Then, thinking back to Anlynne's instructions and following them, Elle felt a rush of warmth through her and the expected item appeared.

She almost broke into a smile at the sense of accomplishment that settled in her but she quelled the urge. However, she could not stop herself from surging forward to the window to check out the supposed color change of her eyes. What she did see was not what she had expected; her eyes were pure silver, not the normal bluish grey or the magical ice blue.

She blinked in surprise and found her iris' as blue as Dan's had been in the morning. Brushing off the previous abnormality as a trick of light, Elle returned to collect the rest of the list before meeting Anlynne.

They sat on her earlier window seat while Anlynne perused the lists, writing down some names on a blank page she had conjured with another flick of her wrist.

"What's that you're writing?" Danielle asked, her recent moment of strangeness forgotten in her interest in whatever her grandmother was doing.

"Just noting down the names of the books that may help. This may take some time, you don't have to sit beside me, but you're welcome if you wish."

Elle simply picked up her book again and sitting next to Anlynne, enjoyed the silent companionship of the older witch.

* * * * *

"Anlynne?"

"Yes?" the older witch looked up from the paper that she had been writing in.

"Could you... Could you tell me about my mother please? I know next to nothing about her, except that I look like her and that she died around a fortnight ago in a car accident." Elle was curious but it felt somewhat awkward to have started this conversation.

Anlynne smiled sadly at her and Elle could imagine the woman thinking about the daughter whom she resembled.

"Well, she left home when she was nineteen so all my memories are of her years here before that."

Elle sighed, "It doesn't matter I just want to know something about her. Tell me whatever you can."

"Let's see. As a child, Melissa was very curious and used to ask so many question that it was a miracle that she didn't drive me to insanity." She let out a watery, reminiscent chuckle.

"Soleus! So many questions that girl had! 'Where is Earth?' 'Why do you control air and not fire like me?' 'Who? What? Why? When? Where?' and her favorite- 'How do Mortaliums, the Lamias who give up magic, live without their powers?'"

Elle watched as Anlynne wiped away a stray tear before continuing. "She was the most kind and caring person you could ever find. I have never seen anyone else who loved as fiercely as she did! When her father died, she was heartbroken, even more than I was and didn't speak to anyone other than her friends for more than a month. She was brave, courageous, and always waiting for the 'next adventure'! I suppose that that's why it wasn't much of a surprise when she left to be a Mortalium before age. She was a fire user you know? Magic for Melissa was as easy as breathing and so, surviving without it was, no doubt, a challenge for her. Oh! She thought it to be the most exciting adventure a Lamia could have- living without magic among the humans."

Anlynne grinned at Elle, and through her, at Melissa, remembering the memories of a daughter she had lost forever but who lived through *her* daughter.

"Melissa loved to read and write, especially poems. Such beautiful poems she wrote! They were never of the same kind and it was as if the words flowed on paper. I remember asking her once about how she did that, and she told me that sometimes a couple of rhyming lines simply popped in her head and when she wrote them down, more and more words came pouring out. She always said that her pen had a mind of its own and that the final draft was so different than what she had started with that she was always surprised at the result." She smiled fondly, caressing Elle's face as she talked of Melissa, and Elle tried not to flinch away, totally engrossed in what her grandmother was telling her.

"She had her quirks too, like always singing something or the other. She used to continually hum something and if by chance you disturbed her, she would hound you to tell her another song. However, what made it even more exasperating was that she never went along with the suggestions and simply thanked you before skipping away, singing a melody unknown to all but her. That was another one of her quirks. She did not like Lamian music much and was always popping over to earth to listen to the latest music that the humans produced."

Anlynne shook her head, her thoughts decades away from the present. "She loved to dance, even though she didn't know how, and whenever I asked her to help me clean, she could be found flouncing about with a duster in hand as if she were a world class ballerina." Danielle smiled at the picture which came to mind at Anlynne's description.

"Melissa was well read and also very helpful and more often than not, it was me who asked for her help rather than the other way round, once she grew up. Oh how I miss my baby girl! It's been a long twenty two years without seeing her face, and now I never will."

Not knowing what to do, Danielle placed a hand on top of Anlynne's and squeezed gently, offering comfort. "You said that you didn't meet her for twenty two years, why? And how did Dan end up here?"

"She made her choice to live with the humans so long ago, and since she gave up her magic, she could not return here. When she had Dan, she asked me to meet her at the Gate, but when I went there, I found just Laurent and Dan there. Melissa hadn't come because she thought that seeing me would hurt. So she stayed away. Laurent gave over Dan to me, and then left. She did come over to spend a day with Dan once a month if she could, in that first year after his birth." Elle felt a pang in her chest as she sympathized with Dan for not having their mother around him as well, but she envied him too, because at least he had actually met her.

Anlynne covered Elle's hand with her own and said, "Even though she is gone, I am thankful to her for making sure that we found you dear. It's as if I have my daughter with me again, well, a quieter version of her, for which I'm blessed." And the two women smiled at the comment, each lost in her own thoughts that anyone could guess, one mourning the death of a daughter and the other, the death of a mother.

* * * * *

They collected and kept the books on a cleared out place at the table and then met Dan in the kitchen for lunch.

After hearing what they had been up to, he said, "Since I don't have to go on a mission anytime soon, I could maybe stay at home to help, though I'll still need to leave for practice. You never know how long it might take to search the library." Anlynne swallowed her mouthful of beans before replying, "However much I dislike you missing classes, I'll admit that this is a greater emergency and I need someone trusted to lend a hand."

Dan just grinned in reply and then turned to face Elle when she asked, "What missions are you talking about?"

"Oh that? Well I am training to be in the Royal Guard. Since threat is low but still present, six guards are assigned to keep the king or queen safe at a time. My friends and I are training to be the next batch when we graduate and the missions are nothing but recon ones to search for more Lamian kids on Earth, the ones whose parents decided to live as humans."

His last words drove her concern over the 'missions' completely out of Elle's mind. Barely in control of her fury, she said, "You carry out missions to take kids away from their parents?"

The coldness in her voice was enough to bring her newfound relatives to a still. Then, Dan gently placed a hand on hers and said, "We don't do it without consent Elle. Every child of Lamian descent is a Lamia and must live in our world till the age of twenty eight when she or he has a choice to either keep their magic or turn Mortalium."

Elle's voice further chilled, "It's still separating a child from his or her parents." and she pulled her hand away, knowing that emotions were flickering across her face through the cracks in her normally well maintained façade, because of her anger.

"Danielle dear, think of it as a boarding school." Anlynne explained in a soothing tone. "The kids live in the palace like royalty! We Lamias love life and value kids more than anything else, and we take good care of them."

"And even with all your love you keep them away from their parents?"

"They get to meet their parents every weekend while studying the rest of the week through. Don't think for a moment that they are unaware of who their parents are." Anlynne explained softly, her tone as if she knew exactly what had hurt her granddaughter. "Well all except Noah, that is." She added as an afterthought.

'There's that Noah again. Who in the world is he?' Elle thought as she let the matter slide for the time being.

The rest of the lunch was spent in a silence broken only by the 'clink' of cutlery against the plates.

* * * * *

The incident at lunch led to Danielle withdrawing from Anlynne and Dan for the day. The two of them knew that she needed some time to think over it and wrap her head around the idea, so they left her alone, researching in the meanwhile.

Danielle walked around the house, exploring the various guestrooms on the ground floor and the unoccupied bedrooms on the first floor which she had not gone in during her first tour, ending up in the gallery. Looking at the way the brush strokes of different shades had come together to form a kaleidoscopic exhibition, showcasing the different moods of the artists, helped calm herself down. She let her thoughts wander within the hues of blues and reds, distracting herself from the words that rang through her mind. *'How to accept someone and something that so casually talked of and did the very things that I despise?'*

Elle spent an hour in the gallery, not really registering the passage of time. When she had looked over every painting in there, committing them all to memory, she felt her mind being invaded by more unwanted thoughts so she went outside towards the summer house through the glass corridor. On paying attention, she noticed that some glass panels acted as doors and opened out to the fields on either side.

Experimentally, Elle gently pushed a 'door', and though it did not budge, her hand passed right through it. Danielle jumped back in surprise, clutching her hand as if burnt. It tingled and she cradled the appendage close to her body and slowly walked forward to examine the erring glass. However, what caught her attention was not the enclosure but the reflection of her eyes which were blazing silver once again. As she concentrated on the color, Elle found her irises suddenly turning blue the moment she thought that it was supposed to be sky-like.

The metaphoric bulb went off in her head and she ran all the way back to the library.

Dan and Anlynne sat up when Elle burst through the door, books and papers scattered around where they were, researching.

They waited till Elle caught her breath, keeping their fruitless notes aside. Danielle said, "Did you find anything on how to change me?"

Anlynne shook her head and replied, "No. There's mention of the Beautiful Ones being able to do it in many books but no directions as to how to actually go about it." She looked disappointed that her precious library had failed her.

Dan could see how Elle's eyes glimmered with barely hidden excitement and he asked, "Why? Did you think of something?"

She nodded and said, "I think I know how. Let me show you."

Anlynne and Dan turned in their seats to face Elle as she walked to the middle of the room, a few yards away from them. Danielle closed her eyes to concentrate as Anlynne and Dan watched her in surprise.

Daniel could not keep his jaw from falling open as he saw the beam of light of the evening sun, entering from the nearest window bend towards Elle and encase her in itself.

It looked as if she had a glowing sheath around her, a transparent covering of light of orange and deep yellow accents. Then, the shell grew gradually more opaque until Elle was completely hidden from sight. With a resounding noise, cracks started appearing on the shell until they covered it in a web of lines which broke it apart and a sudden gust of wind made the shell disappear into nothingness and where Elle had previously been standing, now stood a girl who could never be mistaken for Danielle Hayes.

She looked young, barely in her twenties, with a roundish face, curly auburn hair which rested on the swell of her bosom and a slightly increased height. When she opened her bright blue eyes, Dan was reminded of a book's character with how large and expressive they seemed. When she smiled at their awe, dimples appeared on her cheeks, making her look even younger.

Anlynne broke out of her daze before Dan and walking up to Elle, touched a crimson ringlet and smiling, said, "Although I have no idea how you did that despite my age and experience, I'm very happy for you, Danielle."

She just smiled slightly in reply.

"Oh Soleus." Dan breathed finally. "How did you do that Elle?"

Danielle shrugged as was customary for her and then winking, replied, "Remember, I'm Myra now."

Water

Now that the appearance dilemma had been sorted, without a logical explanation anyways, Anlynne, Dan and Danielle (disguised as Myra) drove to the only school in the valley, simply called the Valley Academy or VA. There were three more schools in Peritia Imperium, one on each mountain as coming down every day was not feasible.

The VA was located near the palace, almost in the center of Peritia Imperium, so as they drove towards it, Elle looked out of the window from where she sat in the backseat, observing the different stores and houses on either side of the paved road, which grew in density as they neared the palace. As the wind made a strand of hair fall into her eyes, Elle raised a hand to brush it off but stopped, observing instead the longer than before fingers of her transformed hand, not yet come to terms with the change.

Elle looked up when the car stopped along with Anlynne and Dan's theories on how Elle might have been able to perform an unknown spell. The VA looked much like the Hayes' mansion, all stone walls with creepers growing on them, the only difference being the background which instead of a forest was now a marble palace with numerous domes and turrets.

The trio climbed out of the car and then Elle followed Anlynne and Dan around the main building to a stand-alone room at the back with a wooden door.

Anlynne said, "Dan, could you go and call Eleza? We need a water user too."

Eleza. The name rang through Danielle's mind like a suppressed memory as she watched Dan nod and walk away. Elle let the thought go and instead focused on the door in front of her, which rivalled the mansion's main doors in height. She could have sworn that it hummed with energy when she touched it so Elle turned to Anlynne and asked, "Magic?"

"Uh huh. Since wood is easiest to imbibe with magic, the door has all sorts of protection spells on it to protect it from accidental magic." Then she opened the door.

The moment Anlynne stepped in, the torches in wall brackets started lighting up till the stone walled room with no windows was fully illuminated. Looking around, Elle said, "Why the lack of ventilation?"

"The room is aired after every test, but since young magic is unpredictable, the glass on windows or even wood would have been damaged. As you can see, the stone would not be harmed and the door has enough spells protecting it."

"Hmm… well, what exactly do I have to do for these tests?" Elle inquired as she ran her hand along a stone basin built in the wall with fresh water filled in it.

Danielle nodded in acknowledgement but by the golden light of the torches, her eyes showed that her thoughts were far away. The name 'Eleza' struck a dull chord in her mind but as hard as she tried, she could not place it. She turned to face the door when she heard Dan's chuckles and found that 'Eleza' looked about 'Myra's' age and was a soft featured blond with characteristic blue eyes. Elle felt that she should know her but then mentally shrugged the notion off and walking forward looked to Dan to introduce them. Elle was sure that her expression matched Eleza's expected one and when combined with Anlynne's amused look she saw Dan's pale visage blush slightly as he suddenly remembered his manners and adorably scratching his head, said, "Right, Eleza, this is E-… sorry, Myra, our new find, and Myra, this is Eleza Steele, one of the most proficient water users of our generation."

Eleza cast a confused glance at Dan before coming forward to shake Elle's hand, "Nice to meet you Myra, seems that despite being older than us he forgets common courtesy sometimes." Elle smiled slightly at Dan's frown at being called the elder one and wondered why the surname Steele rang a bell, but then realized that Eleza had asked her a question, "How were you undiscovered for so long?"

Before Elle could form a reply, Anlynne beat her to it, "Well her father is a human who didn't know that her mother was a Lamia and since the latter died during childbirth, Myra here had no idea that she was a witch and was living in New York when she was found. Thankfully we discovered her." This was said with so much of conviction in it that if Elle did not know the truth and was good at reading people most of the time because of her lie-hating nature, she would not have seen the slight wince as Anlynne spoke of her daughter's supposed cause of death. In spite of her hatred of lies, Danielle could not help but admire the ease with which Anlynne handled the situation. This did, however, make her wary against her grandmother.

Eleza reached out as if to hug Danielle in sympathy but stopped when Dan placed a hand on her shoulder and Elle took a step back. "You're so much like Noah." She chuckled.

Elle could not stand not knowing any longer and asked, "Who is he?" She glanced at her family. "I've heard mentions of him being similar to me but nothing of his actual identity."

Eleza smiled, "Well he's my older brother isn't he? Not technically, of course, but we consider each other to be our siblings. He isn't here at the moment but I'll take you to meet him when he returns. Deal? He's twenty eight though so don't even think of hitting on him, he'll probably see you as another younger sister." She said with a wink. "And well, I say that you're like him because even though he's been here his whole life, according to people, something happened and he changed from a playful child to a quiet one at the age of five.

He also doesn't like to talk to strangers, though you might not feel it, and he too doesn't like physical contact much. The whole time that I've been here, he's been like this, but I can now say that he isn't like that around me anymore. I do want to sometime meet the person whom he might have been if whatever changed had not. So yeah, there you go. That's all Noah's about, and if you want to know anymore, you'll just have to ask him yourself!"

Elle's mind marked Eleza's overuse of 'Well' but her thoughts were occupied with the implicated meaning. She heard Dan snort and then Anlynne cleared her throat as if to remind them of her presence and the fact that they were there for a reason other than exchanging pleasantries.

"Oh yes, let's get started." Eleza said, rubbing her palms together and practically bounced to the basin as she said, "I hope that you're a water one Myra, I need a girl-friend my age."

Elle hid a smile at the age comment and then moving towards Eleza carefully watched what her task was to be.

Eleza closed her silvery blue eyes to open them again revealing bright blue irises and Elle watched as drops of water rose from the basin and hovered above her outstretched palm.

The number of drops rising increased rapidly till it seemed as if minute streams were flowing upwards. Then the flow of water stopped and what was left was a sphere of water floating gently above Eleza's raised hand. She turned her hand upside down and the fluidic ball moved down, eventually mixing with the water in the basin. Eleza grinned at Elle and said, "And that Myra is what you have to do."

Elle felt nervous and cast a glance at Dan who said, "It doesn't make a difference if you are not able to do it Myra, there are two more elements to go." Anlynne added, "But if you are able to do it try to hold the spheres form for as long as you can because that shows your level of proficiency for the element."

"Okay." Elle breathed as Eleza stepped back to give Danielle space to work as Dan and Anlynne looked on with interest.

Elle shut down all of her thoughts to focus better on her task and remembering how she had performed magic earlier, concentrated on what she wanted to happen and surprisingly, a few drops rose off the surface. However they fell back when Dan said, "We never had a water user in our family did we grandma?"

"That is not quite true, my grandmother Liana was one, but as she choose to be Mortalium, I guess that can be excepted."

Danielle was going to question her family but Eleza stopped her. "Concentrate Myra. If you are a water lamia, your level of strength has to be checked for us to see who would be appropriate as a mentor for your skills."

Elle nodded in reply and ignored Dan and Anlynne's discussion which suddenly ceased. Her thoughts of clear and cool running water of a mountain stream collecting in a lake had made a ball of water hover above her palm in a way similar of that of Eleza's.

The three onlookers broke into appreciative applause at how quickly she had gotten the hang of it and Eleza said, "Good. Now let's see how long you can hold it. I'll do it along with you so that we can measure your skill level against mine."

Elle blinked slowly in acknowledgement and concentrated harder to keep her sphere's shape as Eleza raised her own, determined to be the best that she could and discovered that it did not need much thought and power, once formed.

Seconds passed with bated breath and slowly everyone relaxed as the seconds turned into minutes. But then, as the time passed, the atmosphere of the room grew tense again with anticipation as to the level of Elle's powers because even though Eleza's sphere was shaking slightly and a light film of sweat coated her forehead due to exertion, Elle's ball of water was perfectly still and it did not look as if she was even trying at all. When Eleza's globe fell down with a frustrated sigh on her part, Dan exclaimed, "Soleus! How powerful *are* you?"

Danielle's lips twitched in a ghost of a smile but then she decided that five minutes into the task, she was getting bored. Shutting off any distractions from around her, Elle gave her full attention to the sphere, and sending a steady flow of power to it, started tweaking it with her magic, transforming it from a globe to finally an eagle made of water, sitting regally over her hand before Elle silently coaxed it to take flight. Gasps from the other three Lamias broke the silence as the eagle flew twice around them and then climbing higher, up to the roof, exploded with a sound similar to that of a waterfall's crash, the droplets suspended in the air for a moment, glittering like diamonds and pearls, before vanishing from sight.

A dropped pin could have been heard in the silence that ensued. Danielle caught the trio staring at her, her family looking horrified and Eleza gone pale as if encountering a ghost.

"What?"

"Elle," Dan began. "You look like Elle, not Myra."

Common

Elle looked at her rechanged hands and then turned to face Eleza with a terrified look in her eyes. However, Eleza had gone white as if all the blood had drained from her after seeing a ghost.

"Eleza?" Anlynne spoke. "We can explain..."

Eleza did not seem to have heard anything as she walked forward, and ignoring Elle's flinch, caressed her cheek with the back of her hand.

Danielle looked flabbergasted and was almost going to ask Anlynne or Dan to explain when a single word from Eleza made her go absolutely still. "Ellie?"

The suppressed memories that had been elusive till then came crashing down on Elle as she remembered the only person who had ever called her that. Memories of a chubby six year old who never could pronounce 'Danielle'. Rare emotions of longing and affection overwhelmed her and choking on an escaping sob as a single tear ran down her cheek, Elle whispered, "Lizzy".

Almost instantly Eleza surged forward and hugged Elle who held her even closer. Between strangling sobs Eleza said, "I thought I'd never see you again. I cried for you...I missed you so much!"

Danielle let go of Eleza and taking her face in her hands, kissed her on the forehead while wiping away her tears and said, "I'm sorry I left Lizzy-bizzy but I had to, you understand that right?"

Eleza let herself lean forward so that her forehead rested on Danielle's shoulder and mumbled, "I got the lie part but did you ever think of me before leaving?"

Letting through a little part of the loving woman she could be, Danielle caressed Eleza's blond tresses and replied, "Leaving you was the only thing I regretted that day. I'm sorry."

Eleza raised her head and gave Danielle a sad smile, "There never was anything to be forgiven Ellie, I just wish we had met sooner."

Danielle smiled back, knowing that her face would be revealing her relief, and then hugged Eleza again.

Their emotionally charged reunion was broken by Dan's, "Anyone going to explain what just happened?"

Eleza and Elle broke away and Elle was going to respond when Anlynne said, "I'm equally interested to know how you knew each other but we must complete our present undertaking first and then we need to have a chat."

Elle nodded while Dan said, "I better be getting a good explanation for my patience."

Eleza laughed and said, "Don't worry Danny-boy it isn't all that interesting." And Dan shook his head at the nickname while grinning at her words.

Anlynne clapped her hands together to draw their attention to herself, getting a bit annoyed that they were getting distracted so easily and so often.

"Ready for air, dear?"

Elle schooled her expression again and stepping towards the center indicated that Anlynne should go on.

Eleza stepped back to where Dan was and Anlynne stood in front of Elle. "Since this is simply a test to check whether you have any control over air, all you have to do is create a breeze."

Saying this she raised her hands on the sides and almost immediately a gentle gust of wind caressed Danielle's skin. She smiled a little at that and then nodded to show that she understood.

Then Elle mimicked Anlynne's earlier pose and just as she had done with water, thought of warm winds in the summers, cool ones near the beach, how they gently touched her and made her smile involuntarily, immediately lighting up her mood. At first she felt nothing and then she heard Dan say, "Maybe air isn't her." which encouraged her on and the air suddenly moved around her and Eleza remarked with a laugh, "Oh it is, it definitely is." as a particular stroke lifted a lock of her hair playfully.

Danielle closed her eyes, wanting to test her limits and as with water supplied a steady flow of magic from within her, which felt like a place of warmth inside her chest, which grew warmer as she extracted more power from it.

"Danielle!" she heard a muffled cry and opened her eyes to see Anlynne, Dan and Eleza cowering near a wall, as a very fast wind, almost storm-like, blew in the room but had not affected her even though all the torches were snuffed and the room was aglow with a strange pulsing white light which she suddenly realized was in time with her own heartbeat. The wind abruptly stopped due to her state of shock and she fell on her knees, quite painfully. Elle cried out as her head hit the ground before she fainted.

* * * * *

It took a solid minute for him to overcome his shock but then Dan rushed to where her crumbled body lay, skidding the last few feet as he stopped to kneel beside her. The other two followed quickly enough and Eleza sprinkled water on Elle's face to bring her back to consciousness.

"Wha- What happened?" she began groggily, lifting a hand to lightly touch her head and grimacing a little at the contact.

In silence, Dan helped her sit up. Elle did not realize what a sight she had made, hovering three feet off the ground, head tilted up and eyes closed, with pure energy crackling around her. Her skin pulsing with the white light which illuminated the room and her dark hair spread like a halo around her head as the wind whipped around her like a personal storm.

He was one of those who laughed at human horror movies and what they depicted about magic but right then he could not deny that his sister looked like a possessed being. Dan shook his head in disbelief and said, "Well it was all good when you first started but when you closed your eyes, I'm guessing to focus?" Elle nodded. "Yeah well then the wind gained speed. A lot of speed. It felt as if we were standing in the middle of a hurricane! It even blew off all the torches. And you... You were hovering Elle! I called out to you but apparently you didn't hear me and then suddenly you started glowing and the white light appeared." He mumbled in the dark, now that the white light had dimmed to nothing, but then with a wave of his hand lit the torches back on. "I wasn't even able to do this because of your bloody wind." He grumbled.

He shrank back a little when she looked at him and then winced as he watched realization dawn on his sister's face that he was afraid of her. Anlynne and Eleza's quick retreat to the wall showed that they all were.

Confusion reigned free as he imagined her debating on how to react. Dan remembered her telling him about the entirety of her teenage spent with people either being scared of her or calling her a freak because of all the things that kept happening around her and hated himself for his unbridled reaction.

"You are a powerful witch dear, even more than King Rusoe himself." Anlynne said when she finally got out of her shock.

Pure bewilderment flashed across Elle's face before she reined it in.

"Isn't this normal?"

Eleza came forward to answer this, "Well it is Ellie but not for a first timer as yourself. Decades of discipline gives such control."

"No wonder mom wanted you hidden." Dan said, quite happy now that the shock and fear had worn off.

"Hidden? Is that why you changed your appearance?" Eleza inquired.

Anlynne said, "Yes well, we will have to think of a way to hide her again won't we?"

Elle suddenly spoke. "I think I got it this time and I'm sure it will hold."

"Well, try child, it will be a miracle if it lasts."

"Wait a moment here!" Dan broke in. "Won't she take the fire test? I mean, I know that we can control only two elements but come on! No one has ever done this in their first ever actual attempt at magic, so what's to confirm if she cannot have powers over all three?"

Anlynne looked skeptical but Eleza said, "Yeah, no harm in trying. Let's do this!" And Dan chuckled at her excitement and then turning to Elle, said, "Ready to play with fire?" Then he winced as Eleza smacked his head.

"What?" She said innocently. "I cannot in good conscience allow Ellie to hear your cliché lines."

Elle chuckled at this along with Anlynne and then smiled when Dan said, "Soleus! You sure are one violent woman."

Eleza pouted before grinning at his words. "Anyways, Elle, try to break records and blow us away with this too?" He winked.

Danielle shook her head at the two and Dan smiled. Then becoming serious again, she said, "What do I have to do this time?"

"Just try to create a fire." Dan smirked as he made a teardrop shaped flame appear on the top of his right index finger's tip which he blew out like a smoking gun's barrel a moment later.

"Show off." Eleza called out.

"Always." Dan grinned back and then turning to Elle said, "Now you try."

* * * * *

'Compartmentalize.' Elle told herself, as she tried to block out what had taken place. *'Self-doubt won't help.'*

Danielle held out her right hand, palm up, focused all her attention in its center and then closed her eyes, knowing that it helped her concentrate. She turned her thoughts to the fire that Dan had created the night before. She thought of the warmth, comfort and the feeling of safety and of home that the fire had instilled in her.

"Impossible." Elle heard Anlynne whisper in awe and Eleza squeal in delight, but banished it from her mind and then opened her eyes. In her hand now resting was a ball of fire, not unlike that of water she had made before.

Her confidence given a boost by this, she thought of a scene that she had seen in a movie some years ago and willed the flame in her palm to obey her mind. Elle heard Daniel's oft repeated "Holy Soleus." falling from his tongue once more at the four dancing figures of fire that formed by the splitting of the original sphere over Elle's palm. She looked at her brother and then smiling softly at his wonder, looked at the figures again. They collapsed in a pool of flames in her hand which steadily grew in volume and then spilled over the edge onto the floor of the room.

Danielle noticed Anlynne, Dan and Eleza moving from the corner of her eyes but paid them no heed. The trio could only look on with an expression of fascinated horror as the seemingly liquid fire formed a circle around Elle and then started forming mounds, one at each of the four cardinal directions. The mounds grew taller and taller, constantly taking shape, until life size versions of the earlier figures stood in the room.

They were formed of fire and held hands as they danced around Elle in a circle, smiles on their flaming faces. The room lit up in their orange glow, which seemed to lower the torches' light with its intensity, casting dancing shadows on the chamber's walls even though they themselves were the sources of the light, making the scene hauntingly beautiful through its fiery glow.

Elle laughed in exhilaration, a sound of contentment that surprised even her. She closed her eyes once again and the figures flickered into nothingness, the room looking dreadfully dull in their absence.

"Elle..." Dan whispered while Anlynne looked shocked. However, Eleza cheered, "That was awesome! Man what would I give to be a fire user right now to learn how to do this." She pouted wistfully but then broke into a grin and coming forward, hugged Elle again. "I don't care that you've been missing for so long big sister, this right here proves that you were born to be a lamia. Yay! My sister's a badass witch!"

Danielle ruffled Eleza's hair with the after-effects of her laugh still on her face in the form of a small smile.

"Wait a minute. 'Big sister'?" Dan exclaimed, looking between Eleza and Danielle's faces as if he were watching a tennis match.

Danielle shrugged and opened her mouth to reply when Anlynne said, "Elle, you said that you could change yourself again and were sure that it would work, right? Well do it now so that we can get back home and find out some answers."

Elle nodded in response and extracted herself from Eleza. Following her instinct, she sang along the tunes of a forgotten lullaby-

"Hide I must in light of what's to come,

And so for this endeavor, someone else I have to become.

Star light, shine bright, help me find relief,

Help me till I be true in my belief."

A scene similar to the one in the library unfolded in that old testing chamber, with the difference that instead of sunlight, the three elements, some water from the basin and the flame of a torch mixed with the air around Danielle, formed a white shield around her and when it broke, Myra stood amongst them once more.

"Ellie, what did you just say?" Eleza asked, still wide eyed at the process.

"Just something that popped into my mind. Why do you ask though? Didn't everyone hear it?"

"No Elle," Dan said haltingly, "We did not hear it, or better still, we did not understand it. All we heard was what sounded like a musical instrument or something, definitely not Latin or English."

"So Ellie, what did you say?"

She repeated the lines and looked at them inquiringly.

Eleza twisted her lips. "Yeah this time it was in English."

Danielle frowned at the implications. How did she speak in some other tongue without knowing it?

Dan and Eleza both looked as if they wanted to ask something else but Anlynne raised a hand to keep them quiet. "I don't know what happened this past hour but by Lorelei I *am* going to find out. Let's go back home and then I'll talk and Soleus forbid anyone speak unless asked to, got it?" Her blue eyes flashed. She looked perplexed by all the events and Elle knew that she had crossed the line of tolerating such unprecedented situations and now Anlynne Hayes wanted explanations, no matter how long it took.

The younger Lamias nodded quickly in response, not wanting to further aggravate her and then the four walked out of the wooden doors.

Family

"Elle? Eleza? Would you please help us understand how do you two know each other?"

Anlynne asked as they settled in their chairs in the living room of Hayes Manor, except Dan who stood, resting against the back of Eleza's chair.

Danielle felt a vaguely familiar feeling of calmness settling over her which disappeared instantly when Eleza growled through gritted teeth, "I respect you Anlynne, so I would really appreciate you not using Suggestion and Compulsion on us."

Dan groaned, "Really Gramma? You've known her for what, fifteen years now? Don't you trust her?"

Anlynne threw him an uncharacteristically icy glare and replied, "Well she didn't mention any sister in all the years that she's been here, what's to say that whatever she tells would be the truth?"

The words 'Don't trust anyone' from Melissa's letter rang through Elle's mind as she looked upon the exchange between a determined Anlynne and a stone faced Eleza, who had stood up. Her hands were shaking on her sides as she clenched them to control her anger.

Glancing over to Dan's panicky expression, Elle watched him mouth 'Do something!' to her.

She placed a hand over Eleza's closed fists and gently pulled her back. Elle broke through before Eleza could say anything and looking straight into Anlynne's still-blue eyes said, "Anlynne, I've known you for less than twenty four hours but even they've been enough for me to grow fond of you, for the sheer acceptance of me that you showed. However, I agree with Eleza here, we promise to be as truthful as possible but in return we need you to trust us and not take advantage of my naiveté regarding magic."

Anlynne nodded once, conceding to the terms and Eleza relaxed back into her chair slowly, Dan placing a comforting hand on her shoulder.

"Eleza was born when I was five and that was the first time that I wondered about my hair color being different from the rest of my family. The question was never answered and my mind was diverted to something else. As she grew up we became great friends and I loved having a younger sister to look after and play with." Elle smiled sadly at Eleza before continuing. "It was all good till seven more years until the moment that I found out I was adopted and in a fit of fury at being lied to, ran away from home, but not before insisting that my former family not look for me. And that was the last time I saw Eleza before today."

Eleza reached over and hugged Elle before wiping away a stray tear and saying, "I know that this may seem outlandish but the day you left was the day that mum left me here."

"Mum's a Lamia?" Elle almost shrieked, disregarding Dan and Anlynne's expressions. Eleza shook her head. "Well, she was, but then she chose to be Mortalium. That's what she told me. Anyway, she brought me here from Washington DC, accompanied me till just out of the Gates, told me how to get here and then left. And believe me, I never met her again. Noah found me wandering on the road and brought me to the palace where I met Dan for the first time and you know the rest."

Elle was still dumbfounded at the revelation that her adoptive mother had been a Lamia and almost missed Anlynne's question. She shoved the many questions that arose and then tuned in to the conversation that was taking place around her.

"Now that your connection is somewhat clear, albeit I confess to still being horrified at what your mother did. I mean, no contact for more than fifteen years and that too with your child? Preposterous!"

"Lynni." Dan warned his grandmother against rehashing the old argument, seeing the look on Eleza's face at Anlynne's words.

She flushed a bit and then clearing her throat continued, "Moving on to a more pressing topic, Elle, sorry, Myra's powers need to stay hidden."

Eleza piped in, "But why? Her powers are even better than Noah's and after training she herself would be able to become the queen!"

Anlynne shook her head and said, "Such test results are unprecedented and this isn't even the full extent of her powers as she isn't of age yet."

"But..."

"Eleza promise not to tell anyone about it." Dan said, gently turning her around by the shoulders to look at her face.

Elle saw the younger witch searching his eyes, perhaps for any sign that told her that he was joking but even from the distance, she could see his mien was absolutely serious and unsurprisingly Eleza nodded before asking quietly, "Can't I tell Noah?"

Anlynne began "No-", when Elle suddenly stood and not paying attention to the room's other occupants, held out her hand.

"What -?" Eleza started when a paper appeared out of thin air and landed in Elle's hand.

"Wicked." Eleza said along with Dan's surprised, "Another one?"

"What does it say dear?" Anlynne asked as Elle put the page away in her jeans' back pocket.

Instead of replying directly to her grandmother, Elle turned to Eleza and said "I have to tell him myself, though I'd love to have you there when I do."

"Really?" All three of them spoke at once but Elle discerned the varying tones. Anlynne's skeptical, Eleza's excited and Dan's was accepting.

"Yes."

Although Anlynne looked like she wanted to ask about the note, she said "Well that's done, so let's have lunch?"

* * * * *

That night, as Elle lay in her bed watching the sky outside her window, she heard a knock.

"Come in." She called out.

"Hey Elle." Dan said as he walked in.

"Hello. Did you want something?" Elle asked without looking at him. She was quite fascinated by the similarities between the Earth's and Peritia's skies.

He walked over to the window and followed her line of sight towards the heavens.

"Nah. Just wanted to wish you a good night. What are you looking at?" he asked.

She nodded to show that she heard but did not answer and continued to gaze outside.

"Hey, what happened?" Dan asked, sitting on the bed near her feet.

She sighed. "Nothing, I couldn't sleep. Nightmares, remember?"

Dan glanced over to where her face was hidden in the shadows and it seemed as if he was about to suggest something when she sat up and continued. "Anyway. I was wondering how the sun and even the constellations are same here as on earth?" it ended up as a question. He let out a laugh as he too looked at the stars, the constellation Orion prominently visible in the mid-September sky.

"Oh yeah, we didn't really explain that part did we?"

She shook her head and finally turned to look at him. She watched as interest bubbled in him and Elle could see how much her brother loved the topic and a smile tugged at her lips.

"Well think of Earth and Peritia as two images superimposed on one another to form a single picture - which was the earth before the separation - in which some things are similar and the others quite different. As with what happened when Peritia was removed from Earth, if you separate the pictures there would still be some similarities between the two, while existing as two different entities also. In the case of Peritia and Earth, the similarities are the sky and the continuation of the elements from here to earth. For example, the stream that flows down from the Aquain Mountains collects in the Sayliene pond, which is also present on Earth, though known by a different name.

"Huh" was all that Elle could say in reply, for even though she understood what he had explained, she did not know what the accurate response would be for such an elaborate description.

"Yup." Dan replied, as he turned to leave. "Night, Elle."

"Dan?" she asked hesitantly as his hand touched the ornately carved door knob.

"Hmm?"

"Could you…Umm. I was wondering if you'd stay. Last night was the best sleep I'd had in years." She turned to face him, but when he gave no indication of an oncoming reply, she began "It's okay if you don't want to, I'll understand…"

Dan stopped Elle's explanation by quickly crossing over the room and sitting down on the rug beside her bed.

"I'll be here till you need me." He whispered as he leant back against the side of her bed.

"Thank you." Elle sighed as she lay back down. With one hand hanging down the side, clasped with her brother's, she closed her eyes in the comfort of her sibling's presence.

"Hey Elle?" Dan whispered after a few moments of silence.

"Hmm?" She turned on her side to look down at his face.

"What did Mum write to you?" his voice was almost pleading as if the thought of hearing from their mother, though no idea how, was something he just could not ignore.

"Promise that you won't tell anyone else about it?"

"Yeah, I could take a Witch's Vow if you wish, then even if I wanted to I wouldn't be able to do so." Dan promised.

Elle sat up once again, her hand still in Dan's, and willed the fireplace to light up. Then turning to the pride filled face of her brother, she said "Do it."

He nodded and then turning fully, clasped both her hands in his and in steady voice chanted, "Votum est promissio mea." thrice and every time their joined hands glowed in the blue color of magic.

Elle felt the wave of magic wash over her and she knew instinctively that the vow was valid.

"What did you say?" she asked when Dan opened his blue-again eyes.

"It could be roughly translated to 'I vow to keep my promise.' Thrice for three promises, to keep my word, to help you, and to be there for you. And since while making it I had promised to not disclose whatever you tell me with relation to mum to anyone, and breaking that promise will lead to severe consequences, making me forever incapable of breaking it again."

Elle had had enough of accepting things without answers. "What consequences? And why in Latin? Won't any other language work? Is magic sensitized to particular sounds for a spell?"

"Hold your horses!" Dan chuckled and Elle felt her cheeks warm, embarrassed at her curiosity.

He shook his head in amusement and dodging away from her playful smack to his arm, Dan answered. "The questions you put forth are quite logical but there answers may not seem so."

"What do you mean?"

"The consequences are different from person to person, from mere loss of voice to insanity to even death, depending on the severity of what revealing the secret might lead to. It is a very serious thing to do and should not be taken lightly. With regards to your question about Latin, mostly magic does not depend upon the spoken words, as was evident when you did the tests.

However in spells which are more specific in function, the caster should be clear in their intent. This is why such spells are usually cast by stating what we want in Latin, a language not commonly used. This ensures that our concentration is maintained throughout the casting, and the spell remains true to its original goal."

"Huh. That makes sense. Kind of." Elle murmured, thinking over the explanation.

"Now if your quest for knowledge is satisfied for now, could we get back to the original track, Mum's letter?"

"Oh, yes!" she fumbled around the bed finally extracting the paper from under the pillow and handed it over to Dan who raised the intensity of the fire to provide more brightness.

"Dear Danielle," Dan read aloud.

"I know that I've been asking a lot from you lately and am also aware that blind trust goes a little way only. Although I regret the lack of exchange of pleasantries, you would, hopefully, agree that getting to the point directly is better than beating around the bush. Also, I was told that my letters to you should contain nothing but what is necessary and so these may seem a bit...blunt. However, I will do my duty of guiding you on the right path and keep you from straying.

My request to you today is that you build a friendship based on trust with Noah and tell him everything that you deem necessary whenever you wish, for he would not betray you.

Also, notwithstanding my love and respect for my mother, try not to tell her everything because she may, albeit unwillingly or even unknowingly, reveal sensitive information to someone who must remain ignorant of you at all costs.

Trust me I want to, but I'm not allowed to explicitly or even remotely tell something you have to discover on your own. I will say this – trust Noah, Dan and Eleza, but be wary of everyone else for they may accidently reveal what must stay hidden.

I've got to go, so bye for now.

Love always,

Melissa.

P.S: Even magical oaths cannot be trusted, so don't go on making them with people other than the three I named to bring them within the circle of knowledge."

"Way to be mysterious Mom." Dan groaned as he handed the paper back to Elle for safekeeping. "But I don't think that we need to worry about the oath right now, because she said that it was okay to tell me, right?"

She nodded in agreement and then lay back down, slipping the paper under her pillow once again.

Suddenly, a line struck her as odd and she took the letter out again. Reading it twice, she nudged Dan and said, "What does she mean by '*I was told that my letters to you contain nothing but what was necessary*' and '*I'm not allowed*'? Who tells her all these things? Better still, how are these appearing anyways?"

Dan frowned, and read it again, "You're right. And now that I think about it, time travel is impossible now. Having magic and the power to change time? It was outlawed hundreds of years before Peritia's creation and the history books say that all the scrolls pertaining to time travel were destroyed too."

"So how is this happening?" Elle threw her hands about to indicate the absurdness of the situation, helpful or not.

"I don't know Elle. I really don't." He flopped his head back on the side of the bed with a frustrated sigh and putting the fire out, plunged the room into darkness once more.

Elle sat up again. "I felt that!"

"What?"

"When you used magic. I can feel it happening before you actually put it to use, I felt you collecting it!"

"Just like you did this afternoon? When you knew the letter was arriving?" Dan asked, curiosity, and some disbelief, evident in his tone.

"Exactly like that! It's like I can feel the energy if it's used near me... wait a minute. If I can feel it coming, maybe next time a letter comes we'll be able to make out the source of the power! Is there a spell to do that?"

"There might be, there's a spell to do almost anything." Dan shook his head. "We'll look for it the next time I have a day off, okay?"

"Fine. Till then I'll hope that nothing else arrives." Elle said resignedly, the sudden excitement seeping out of her voice.

"Wonder how she knew Eleza and Noah's names though..." Dan mumbled before closing his eyes, fingers tightening around Elle's as she snuggled further into the bed, returning his actions with a squeeze of her own.

Sisters

The next day, Elle took out time to explore the house. She found that it was not actually as huge as she had originally assumed, not that it was small by any means. The main structure's floor plan was almost square-ish in shape, with the width of the house as seen from the gate being smaller than the depth. The library took the entire left side, a fact that made Elle wonder how long it would take her to finally get through all of its treasures. A wide corridor stretched from the entrance to the staircase leading upstairs, which also hid the backdoor leading through to the 'Vitrum Andron' or the glass corridor which ran through the garden.

To the right of the great doors of the entrance, lay two archways, the one nearer to the door leading to the drawing room. It was a beautifully decorated chamber, with walls painted a soothing blue, the outer wall, having the windows, a shade darker than the other three. The heavy draperies and the upholstery on the pale ash-wood couches and the chaise longue, along with the other knick-knacks decorating the room, all exuding an aura of luxury. Elle liked the room, but did not feel very comfortable in the too-formal setting, and often moved to the adjacent living room.

The living room lying beside the drawing room, if one faced its entrance, looked like a negative of a photograph of the latter. Its archway provided a good view of the walls painted a warm brown, with maple furniture and the plushy dark blue carpet, which just invited all who saw it to remove their shoes and sink their feet in the carpet's decadent softness. It was a beautiful room and much of Dan and Elle's conversations took place in there, both of them lounging on one couch each.

As Elle entered the dining room, one of her earliest impressions of it, along with its consequences rose to mind. The room's main wall that was unbroken by doors was adorned by beautiful China plates. Each gold rimmed piece of crockery had a flower hand-painted on it and they looked quite real, in Elle's opinion at least. During the first meal that she had in that room, Elle discovered the fragile plates that were so nonchalantly used by Anlynne for serving the food in. The cutlery too was actual silverware and she could not bring herself to use the delicately carved utensils to eat something as mundane as pasta. Anlynne noticed this and for easing Elle, Dan and her had since then took to having meals on the large island in the center of the kitchen where they ate in 'normal' plates and with 'normal' stainless steel cutlery.

The library was a place that held the most of Elle's interest and most of her next week was spent with Elle reading the books pertaining to the introduction to Elemental Magic, playing the piano in the music room on the first floor, spending time in the gallery and the 'Vitrum Andron' or the 'glass corridor'. Dan unfortunately could not get the time off to help her with the research for the letters, so most of Elle's free time was spent catching up with Eleza either in the back garden or while walking through town, always disguised as Myra.

Even though they were not actually related, and had spent fifteen years apart, the two witches considered each other's to be sisters still. Elle remarked on this, Sunday afternoon, as they strolled near the summerhouse, enjoying the slightly chilly breeze that blew over the nearby pond.

"Hey Lizzy, if we are sisters according to you, and Dan is my brother, then won't 'you and Dan' be considered incest?" Elle emphasized 'you and Dan' with air-quotes, with a smile playing on her lips. This earned her a playful shove to her shoulder as Eleza blushed and murmured, "Shut up Myra." All the people who were in on the secret tried to use Elle's chosen name rather than her given one to make it seem normal as practice for when they would meet others.

Elle let out a laugh, a slowly common becoming reaction of hers, and raising her hands in the universal gesture for 'I come in peace', justified herself.

"What? Do you really expect me to believe that there's nothing between the two of you? 'I can see a church by daylight' you know."

"Stop quoting Shakespeare, you bookworm." Eleza groaned. "Though I hereby declare you as not-my-sister, in light of your recent words of surprising wisdom." She added mischievously.

Ignoring the latter part of Eleza's reply, Elle said, "Pot-kettle-black? How would you have caught the reference if you hadn't read the play yourself?" She retorted, and in a moment of childishness, threw the small bunch of wild flowers that she had gathered at Eleza. The younger witch squealed and ran away, with Elle close on her heels. Suddenly the elder one called out, "Lizzy!"

Eleza turned around as Elle stood still. She ran over and asked, "What happened Ellie?"

"Magic." Elle whispered. "There's magic headed this way."

"How-?" Eleza began and broke into a grin just as Elle gasped, when leaves fallen from a nearby tree blew towards them, hovering in the air, forming a face like structure which spoke in a man's lovingly gentle and happy voice, "I'm back sis." And the leaves collapsed at their feet.

"What was that?" Elle enquired, after her shock wore off, picking up one of the fallen leaves and examining it. She could, somehow, feel the magic as it seeped out.

Eleza rolled her eyes, "It is stupid how easily I forget that you weren't always here. That, my dear Myra, is how we communicate in Peritia. You see, cell networks don't work here, obviously, and running around ourselves or even sending someone else, takes a lot of time.

So the plants become our mode of communication. Heard of the phrase 'though the grapevine'? It becomes real here. Anyways, a simple spell, 'Tralatio' which means 'transfer', is enough and all that you need to do then is speak the person's name and your message and the leaves, or flowers, will relay your message. And since there are plants everywhere in Peritia, it's a pretty quick and efficient method. The magic flows from plants through soil to the fallen leaves which finally assume life for a few moments to convey the message. Got it?"

Eleza's rambling was as endearing as it was informative and Elle smiled a little while nodding slowly as she pondered over it. She remembered a movie that she had shown the children in her class some years ago, in which flower petals relayed information in a somewhat similar way.

"Won't it be a terribly public way to communicate? What if the information we need to send across is not meant for all ears?" Her mind spun, thinking about everything that she had to keep secret from almost everyone, if her mother's instructions were to be followed.

The younger witch grinned, "No. Just add 'Celatum', which loosely translates to 'concealed', at the end of your words. It would ensure that the words be heard by the intended hearer only as dust becomes the carrier then and no one is the wiser about whether something was relayed or not, except for the one receiving it. Well, the receiver and you it seems. How in the Realms were you able to sense that coming?"

Elle shrugged. "I don't know, felt a tingle, not unlike the one I felt when my mother's letter arrived."

"Hmm..." Eleza mused, but instead of pondering over an explanation for it, said, "Well, give it a try why don't you?"

Elle quirked an eyebrow at Eleza's apparent excitement and then following the latter's instructions, said, "Tralatio; Daniel Hayes. Hello Dan, Elle here, hopefully learning something new from your wanna-be girlfriend today, hopefully. Celatum."

Eleza made a face at Elle when she heard this but Elle did not pay much attention to that.

Instead, she observed the blades of grass near her feet rustle in a sentient sort of way and she could almost feel the magic flowing from her into the ground through the plants.

"Now what?" Elle finally turned to Eleza who had apparently stopped trying to bring her outrage at Elle's words to her notice, when she realized that her not-sister was not listening.

She smiled. "Now we wait to see if-"

The same grass blades as before along with a few fallen white flowers rose up and in Dan's voice, spoke, "Hey Elle, glad to see and hear your progress. Sorry I'm a bit busy right now, but we'll celebrate later. Oh! And Eleza, wanna-be girlfriend huh?" his laughter faded as the messengers lost their powers yet again.

"He'll never let me live that one down." Eleza groaned. "Really Ellie, my own sister?"

"You were the one who renounced me remember?" Elle winked and then ruffled Eleza's blond hair. Laughing as her hand was batted off, she continued, "That boy just loves to celebrate doesn't he? In a week of my being here, I've been subjected to celebrating my own 'home-coming', Lynni's successful rearrangement of the library upstairs and also his own completion of twenty two and a half years of life! I mean seriously?"

"Yup that's Dan, and you never can back out of his plans." Eleza nodded solemnly. "What with those eyes and those dimples." She added, her mind seemingly miles away.

"Hey! Stop thinking about my brother." Elle mock frowned at her on-and-off sister.

"Oh!" Eleza suddenly smacked her forehead. "Speaking of brothers, let's go meet Noah in the palace!"

"What?"

"Who else do you think sent me that message? Noah's back from Earth! And I've missed him so much. I haven't seen him in months as he was off training in the Aquain and then the Fyrie Mountains before leaving for Earth. Didn't I tell you that I called him my brother?"

Eleza shook her head in mock disappointment at Elle's inattention. "Ooh... and maybe Aunt Maebel and Uncle Rusoe would also be home!"

"You, my dear, have a lot of fake family members." Elle laughed.

"Well my real ones left me so what was I supposed to do?" The younger witch mumbled after a few seconds of silence.

Elle surprised the both of them when she stepped forward and wrapped her sister in a loving hug.

"It is said," she whispered. "That love of any form can only be given if it has been received at least once. This was how you held me when we were younger and it's all I know of comfort." Elle's words though talking of something else, were said in a tone that conveyed how much she regretted leaving Eleza behind and also of how much she loved her 'sister'.

Eleza sniffed once, stifling a sob as she gently moved away, the broken smile on her face a sign of forgiveness. Then, letting out a choked laugh, she tried to lighten the mood. "Let's go meet Noah then? After all, he is to be your instructor."

Elle was wiping away Eleza's tears when she stiffened, "What do you mean 'instructor'?"

"Oh just that Noah was the most powerful yet-to-mature Lamia around and was supposed to become the king when he came of age magically and Uncle Rusoe's century was over. Note the emphasis on 'was' as now it seems that we'll be having a queen next, what with your already super awesome pre-maturity powers!" Eleza said airily as if announcing her sister's ascent to the throne was a normal topic for her.

"Wait a second. What do you mean by pre-maturity powers? Lynni's brother-in-law is the king?! And what was that bit about his 'century' being over?" she almost exploded with curiosity sprinkled with irritation.

"Whoa! Slow down, would you?" Eleza chuckled. "Let's walk to the palace, it's only a couple of miles away and I'll answer your questions to the best of my abilities."

Danielle gave her pseudo-sister a look that clearly stated how much she preferred having her answers then and there but would agree solely because she had no choice.

Eleza caught her hand and giving it a tug, started running towards the backdoor of the house through the glass corridor, calling back to Elle, "Last one to the main gate tells Noah your secret!"

Half amused and half annoyed, Elle ran after the one person whom she loved most in that world. She ran with just one thought in her mind, *'Hell will freeze over before I'd willingly tell my life story to a complete stranger!'*

Storm

Storms. Brown-turning-grey skies, cool, swift winds and the feeling of anticipation that hung thick in the air for the oncoming rain. Sitting cross-legged in the Vitrum Andron, Danielle let out an amused chuckle remembering the few light-hearted romantic comedies that she had read and watched. Most of them had at least one storm scene, wherein, the heroine being scared of thunder and/or lightening is comforted by the male lead. How clichéd. She commented mentally.

Astraphobia really did seem unnatural to her, a person who loved watching storms from gathering to dissipations. Thunder shook the ground and lightening pierced the sky while icy waters rained down, enthralling her. Getting up, she shed her jacket and with a slight push opened the door nearest to her, stepped out and closed it behind her.

Elle reveled in the first drops that touched her skin. She spread her arms and looked to the sky, just as another streak of electric blue flashed across it. She closed her eyes and opened her mind, concentrating as Eleza had had taught her. Suddenly, she felt her consciousness expand, encompassing her surroundings, feeling every single drop that fell on the leaves of trees, blades of grass and petals of flowers in the back-garden. She felt them as if they were falling on her own self. Some drops slithered down from where they had fallen, dripping to the ground and then being soaked up by the parched land. Others lingered on, nestled inside the depths of flowers, collected in greater numbers, weighing the flower down so much that water pour out splashing down, the flower straightening again with the weight now gone, ready to collect newer drops. Elle could feel the spray that formed clinging to the sticky spider webs, making them look as if adorned with gems.

She smiled as another drop fell on her face and sliding across her cheek and down her neck, was absorbed by the collar of the shirt she wore. Elle was fully aware that the pale pink cloth had gone translucent in the rain, but did not care a whit. She opened her eyes then, but when she saw the grey color of the clouds, a color so common in Peritia's residents' eyes, all that she could think of was one person. A person whose name she now breathed out in a soft whisper, "Noah."

* * * * *

Eleza and Elle's race had ended with Elle, even as Myra, won. Breathing heavily, she laughed as she clutched her sides.

"Looks like you lost kiddo."

Eleza smirked, "More like I let you win." And then in a moment reminiscent of their childhood, stuck out her tongue before breaking down in giggles.

"You done?" Elle raised an eyebrow at her 'sister' who grinned and said, "Nah, but I'll stop."

Elle shook her head and started off towards the garage where the cars were parked. "Hey Myra!" Eleza called. "Let's walk? That way I can answer your questions today."

Danielle shrugged in reply and then followed Eleza, walking out of the premises. As they ambled down the main road, Eleza said, "Your questions were regarding the pre-maturity powers, King Rusoe and the century rule right?"

Elle nodded and waved her hand, inviting Eleza to continue.

"Let's start with the pre-maturity powers. You know Lorelei's story? Well, since she got her powers at the age of twenty-eight, the trait became hereditary, and all the Lamias got their full powers at that age, which is known as the maturity age."

"But-?" Elle began.

"How can we do magic?" Eleza smiled. "Well these powers that we have currently are half of our total magic, a result of another of the Beautiful Ones' spell. They made it so, so that we may have some grasp of how to use our magic, following some truly gruesome incidents where all the powers came suddenly. To access the full powers, a Lamia is given a Token, which is essentially a way to tap the magic and control it with better ease. However, Tokens sap magic the longer they are worn and it is advised not to sleep while wearing it, but we'll get to that when you actually need it."

"So my actual magic capacity is even higher than my current one?" Elle wondered aloud.

"Yup. And not just higher, double of your current ones. Which is why I said that you might be the next queen?" Eleza explained.

"I still don't get it."

"This leads to you next question- King Rusoe, and the century rule too." Eleza continued.

"Here in Peritia Imperium, there are two levels of government. One is the Council which consists of one member each of the First Families- Allen, Ayres, Baldwick, Hayes, Simms and Wyndstor. The other is the Monarch. Every Monarch has a reign of hundred years, which may be cut short either by death or by the Council, though the Council has intervened only once and that was during the reign of Charlotte the Cruel, when she was dethroned and then executed for her crimes against both Lamias and the Mortalium. Anyway, so the next Monarch is the most powerful Lamia present. Only twice has a Monarch been re-elected, once with King James, and then again with Queen Runél. Want to know a not-so-secret? Even though she ruled just before King Rusoe who has now been king for ninety-five years, I haven't found a single painting of her in Peritia."

Elle thought over this as they walked through the market, and then asked, "Where do I fit into this?"

"See, before your arrival, Noah was the most powerful, pre-mature Lamia, and it was sure that he would be the next

Monarch when he came of age and Rusoe retired. So, in spite of his wishes, he has been training to be the next Monarch under Rusoe's wing ever since he could learn. Now, with your arrival and your awesomely amazingly unprecedented powers, you automatically became the new heir to the throne. Though I can't fathom why your mom wants you to stay hidden."

"Maybe it's because of this?" Elle mused.

"Maybe." Eleza hummed. "Hope I answered all your questions?"

"For now." Elle sighed. "It's more complicated than I thought. But, since we're here at the palace, I'll stop."

Eleza grinned as they entered the foyer of the huge building, moving through the corridors, completely at home. "Come I'll show you my room and then we'll go meet Noah!"

Elle smiled at her enthusiasm, and then unwillingly tearing herself away from the beautiful tapestries, painting and statues that adorned the corridors, she followed Eleza to another wing of the Palace.

"These are the dorms." Eleza said, gesturing as they walked. "This is where all the kids, those whose parents decided to be Mortaliums, stay. There's a Rec Hall, which unlike those of earth, since electricity isn't transmitted here, consists of a small library, along with board games for the entertainment of the students. And this," She pointed to the right. "Is my room." She opened the door to a twelve by twelve room, with a characteristically huge window with an expanded sill on the right, and a door, presumably leading to a bathroom, on the left. The wall having the window was a deep purple while the other three were lavender in color. In front of the entrance lay a simple bed with a black and purple bedspread, with a black coverlid. A small and quaint rug lay between the bed and the cupboard to the left, with a small bookshelf near the head-end of the bed.

"Like it? It's been mine for all these years and has seen a transition from hot pink to yellow and now to a purple theme." Eleza grinned, though her face contorted in a slight grimace at the mention of 'hot pink'.

Elle laughed at her expression and then said, "It's a great place to have to yourself in the palace Lizzy." Eleza smiled at the nickname and then said, "Come on, let's go find Noah. And tell him all about you!" Elle pouted slightly which made Eleza smirk as she said, "Don't worry, he's good looking enough to compensate for the loss of your secrecy with him." And she dodged the pillow that Elle threw at her.

* * * * *

They wandered through the palace, with Eleza stopping to greet someone or the other every once in a while. It was in the east wing, near the throne room when Eleza exclaimed, "There he is!" pointing to two men standing at the end of the corridor, one facing them, and the other away. The former looked to be Elle's age with sandy blonde hair, sharp features and about six feet tall. At Eleza's greeting the man facing them broke into a smile and waved to her, rolling his fingers in the universal gesture of 'I'll talk to you later'. Danielle, however, was not paying attention to that because she had felt *a sharp pain on the back of her neck. In a fraction of a second the area had grown burning hot and then ice cold before turning back to normal. She gasped at the sensations and felt as if there was a thread pulling her towards where the men stood, and she tugged sharply at Eleza's hand, eliciting an 'Ouch!' from the younger Lamia. What she failed to notice, was Noah's similar reaction.*

The utterance drew the other man's attention and he turned to face the women. He looked to be in his thirties in normal human age, but Elle knew that he must have been at least one and a half centuries old. He had dark brown hair which rested atop his roundish face that somehow held an edge to it. Even from the distance, Elle could discern the calculating cold look his eyes cast, despite his overall welcoming appearance. His cool expression faltered for a moment before returning back to politely curious and Elle could have sworn that the uncontrolled moment had revealed a stone-splitting rage but then she chalked up her thoughts to be a reaction to whatever she had felt.

The sense of unease grew under his gaze, and in spite of being disguised as Myra, Elle tugged at Eleza's hand once again, though lightly, trying to convey her wish to leave. Eleza misinterpreted her actions and slightly pulling Elle along, walked over to where the others were standing.

Making a small curtsey in front of the older man and then hugging Noah quickly, she said, "Good morning, Your Majesty. May I introduce, Myra Mills, a new friend of mine."

Noah merely gave her a cursory glance while the other man, who was apparently King Rusoe, put his hand out in greeting. *"Pleased to meet you dear, though it's quite unusual to find a new recruit who is so grown up. I'm afraid that the name Mills is not one that I am able to place."* His sentence sounded like a question that Elle was not sure as to how to answer.

Eleza intervened. *"Your Majesty, she was found just a few weeks ago by Daniel Hayes on one of the recon missions. She was an orphan with no name, who lived on the streets so she made up one herself when the police authorities questioned her. Moving from place to place in foster homes, it is surely not that surprising that she remained undiscovered for so long."*

Elle would have scoffed aloud at the fast spun tale if her heart had not been beating that hard against her rib cage.

The king nodded at the explanation, though he still looked somewhat perplexed but he let it go. Then, he said to Eleza, *"What is up with this 'Your Majesty' talks? How often do I have to tell you kids to call me Uncle Rusoe? Indulge an old man his whims till the time you are staying in the palace at least."*

"Yes Uncle." Eleza smiled.

"Now give this uncle of yours a hug and then get away from my sight. I'll send Noah over when I'm done with our work." He said, mock annoyance in his tone.

Eleza laughed and complied with his wishes and then throwing a quick smile at Noah, guided Elle out of the room. Once out of earshot she turned to Elle and frowned, *"What happened Myra? Why did you freeze up like that?"*

Elle looked down as she said, "I don't know Lizzy, I'm just not that good with strangers." Knowing that her actual reason of her discomfort sounded farfetched, she left it at that.

"Well get used to him because one, he is the king, and two, he is a part of your family, even though he doesn't know it yet. Do you reckon we should tell him?"

Panic, hot and fast, surged through Elle at these words. "No!" she almost shouted. "Promise me Eleza; promise me that you won't tell him."

"Whoa! Calm your horses. Okay. Okay I won't tell him." Eleza said, before adding, "Though it can be considered treason to keep things from the king."

"I know that, but just...don't alright? Not until I say so." Elle almost pleaded, making a mental vow that she would never say so.

"Alright." Eleza conceded and Elle let out a sigh of relief.

"Now let's head back to the Manor, Noah will let us know whenever he is free. Most probably our walk over made us late to catch him in time."

Elle nodded in agreement, though only half paying attention to the younger witch's words, her mind already wandering with the mention of 'Noah'.

* * * * *

Elle sighed as the light dimmed further and the color of the sky grew darker, with the rain falling harder, and she made her way back in; the wards on the back door drying her clothes. Eleza had told her earlier that she would tell Noah the basics and then have him come over with her in the morning before Dan left so that the four of them could have the much needed yet postponed chat. She trudged up the stairs, dreading as well as welcoming the next day, because although she still was not comfortable with sharing the details with a stranger, knowing that it was Noah made her feel better. Though, laying down in her bed, her hand clasped once again in Dan's as he lay on the mattress he had transferred into her room after dinner, Elle could not help but wonder why she had been fixating so much on him and why the feeling was being lessened every passing moment.

Looking back on the day's events, another memory triggered her thoughts to divert once again. This time they made their way to dinner although not the meal itself as the conversation that had taken place in its preparation had been far more interesting.

* * * * *

After coming back from the palace Danielle had changed into an old pair of faded blue jeans, and a long sleeved black shirt. Wearing any of her mother's dresses remained an uncomfortable notion to her still. She then made her way down to the kitchen where Anlynne was preparing the food.

She was singing softly as she worked, facing away from the door, and Elle simply stood at the doorway and observed. Elle could make out the ties of the pale blue apron that the older witch was wearing, over a knee length white dress, patterned with pink flowers. Her hair had been pulled up into a bun to reduce interference in her work. This drew Elle's attention to the fact that Anlynne's nape was glowing. It was not quite discernable but it seemed as if there was a symbol as the center of the glowing patch of skin.

Curious, Danielle knocked on the doorframe to make her presence known and walking over, gestured to Anlynne to hand over the knife she was using to chop salad. "Let me help."

"Oh sure dear." Anlynne let go with a smile and instead, turned to prepare the chicken, which was apparently on the menu that night.

As Elle chopped, she smiled softly at Anlynne's quietened humming beside her and wondered how to broach the topic. Then, "Did it hurt?"

Anlynne looked at her confusedly, "What did?"

"When you got that tattoo, the one on the back of your neck. Did it hurt?"

"Oh that!" Anlynne absently caressed the spot in question. "It isn't a tattoo dear, it's my love bond."

"Your what now?"

Anlynne washed her hands at the sink, drying them off on her apron, after having set the chicken to marinate. She smiled at Elle's bemusement and explained. "Lamias don't get married. Not the way the humans do, anyways. Have you seen any church here? Or any other place of worship really?"

Elle shook her head slowly as she sifted through her little knowledge of Peritia mentally, coming up with nothing.

"You see, when Lamias get 'married' the ceremony is known as a bonding and not a wedding. It's mostly held at midnight, according to the belief that then is when Soleus' temperament is least likely to affect it, and the Queen is at her most benevolent."

"The Queen? Who's that? Lorelei?" Elle asked, more than slightly confused.

"No not Lorelei, it isn't actually mentioned who she is. Some texts say that she is the Queen of the Universe. The Keeper of everything there is. But some say that she is not even been crowned yet. I remember being fascinated by the concept, how could we ask for someone's blessings when we aren't even sure of her existence?" Anlynne shook her head.

"There was a passage I read, many years ago, it went something like- 'The Universe lies in wait for its Timeless Queen and when the time will arrive for her to ascend the throne, a hidden battle will wage between Good and Evil, one who will stop at nothing to let her claim her right, the other who'll do all they can to prevent it from happening. Though all of this, the Queen must be kept unaware of her True Identity, and must be kept from Evil, lest she lose

her destiny.' Didn't understand it then, don't understand it now."

Elle felt her brow pull together in a frown at the words even as Anlynne continued. "Anyway, I got away from the topic on hand. The bonding, entails a few vows and an Ancient Spell, and the proof of its completion is the appearance of this mark." Maneuvering so that Elle could see it, Anlynne exposed her bond-rune to her.

Now able to look closer, Elle saw a symbol that looked like two superimposed infinity symbols, save for the fact that they were incomplete. The left half of both of the horizontal '8's was not fully drawn. She tried to make sense of their meaning but being unable to do so, she asked, "Why are they incomplete?"

Anlynne chuckled as she turned back to face Elle, "That is to signify that even though we are immortal, love might not always exist between the same two people and so the bond is not permanent and can be broken if need arises. It's a safety feature, if you wish to put it like that."

"Safety feature? How?"

"You see, being bonded serves as a source for additional powers, some which may prove to be harmful if one wishes to use them for wrong purposes. This isn't just a rune. It's a magical rune. People who are bonded through it gain the ability to know the vague whereabouts of their partners, gauge their emotions, things like that. The Bonded share their magic and it is shared proportional to their needs at a given point. So you see how this can be troublesome?"

Elle nodded, and then asked, "How come yours is still there? Not to sound insensitive, but I remember you telling me of his demise."

Anlynne smiled and Elle caught the sadness lurking in her eyes. "He died two scores ago. Over expenditure of magical energy while he was renewing the wards to this old place." She shook her head and then continued with her pseudo lesson. "The mark isn't always visible, see?" and she revealed a rune-less neck to Elle.

"And why is that?"

"It only appears when you're thinking of you Bond Mate. You see, your grandfather loved my cooking." She offered in explanation.

Danielle did not know what to say, so she changed the topic, watching Anlynne surreptitiously wipe away a stray tear of remembrance.

"You made me realize that I did see no places of worship here. Are there actually none, or did I miss them?" Elle asked, because even though she had never felt an inclination to pray, she loved examining the beautiful stained windows of the church and the quiet serenity that every place of worship offered.

"That's somewhat hard to explain," Anlynne began. "You see, since childhood, we are taught to take full responsibility for all our actions and any consequences that they might have. Blaming someone, or something, whose existence cannot exactly be proved is...just not done. I know that this

seems hypocritical in face of Soleus and the Queen, but we only believe in Soleus because there are official records of his existence, and the Queen, well she is more of a legend or a bedtime story for anyone to actually believe anything about her. It's my belief, and most of the other Lamias' too that it is better to think before you act or speak, rather than repenting after it's already been done. One must never be ashamed of their actions because if they are, they should never have done it in the first place itself." She finished simply.

Elle nodded in acquiescence as this resonated with her own philosophy. Not that she was against anything, she lived by the motto of 'live and let live', allowing everyone the freedom of opinion, even when it differed from hers. She too believed that all good and bad that had happened to her, especially after she started college, was a result of her own actions, her own hands' work, and she could not bring herself to thank, or blame, what seemed like a non-entity, for it.

Dan's entry into the kitchen and his exclamation of, "I knew that it was chicken I smelt!" put a stop to her mind's wanderings and Elle had turned to chopping up the salad once more.

* * * * *

Elle snuggled deeper into her pillow, and welcomed Morpheus' comforting arms, as sleep overtook her will to stay awake and she drifted off into the land of dreams.

* * * * *

While Elle had been standing in the rain outside, a very important meeting was being held in the Throne Room in the palace, where six men knelt in front of the throne. The figure which sat on the throne wore a black cloak, which looked as if it were made of shadows.

"Tell me, Zeke." The figure spoke softly, the voice in morbid contrast with the cruelty that flashed in the eyes whose color fluctuated between blue and pure black. 'Zeke' clutched at his throat as he felt the air lessening around his face, unable to breathe as if he were drowning. His followers knelt in perfect silence which must have been in total contrast to their thoughts as they watched their leader being punished.

"Tell me how Melissa Hayes is still alive."

Loss

The other five of the original six who knelt, excepting Zeke, watched as their companion elicited one last choking sound before finally succumbing to their Master's anger.

The figure's eyes, which had taken a static black color, now reverted to their original fluctuating state as Zeke lost his fight with Death.

"Charlise." He spoke, sounding not even the slightest bit bothered by the body of his dead servant lying at his feet, his tone light, almost mocking.

The second last kneeling figure bowed further and murmured, "Yes, Master?"

"See that you do not make your mate's mistake. She is here under the guise of a Myra Mills. Either subdue her and find out about her child, or prepare to soon be united with your group's former leader."

"I will not fail master." She announced clearly, no doubt evident in her tone.

"For your sake, I hope you prove to be right in your presumption. Step forward."

She got up, not looking at her dead husband's figure, walked up to the throne and raised her chin as the Lamian sign of submission.

The cloaked figure rose, and taking out a black blade from within the lifeless Zeke's cloak-folds, held it against her exposed throat. Applying enough pressure to make a nick and draw blood, he spoke aloud, "Kneel my servant, the new leader of the Guard. Kneel, for I have spared you today, and serve, knowing that I hold your life's thread in my hand."

Charlise knelt, and as her hand accidently brushed Zeke's fallen figure, a single tear fell from her eye, the sole sign of grief in her statue like demeanor.

* * * * *

Slowly the light in the room brightened and the cloak of the figure on the throne solidified, the color appearing to be a royal purple instead of the earlier black.

"Elmor."

"Yes Master?" another one of the kneeling Guards spoke.

"Go bring Noah here. Since we are short of a Guard due to these…unpleasant circumstances, I believe that the time for his initiation has finally arrived."

"Very well, Master." And Elmor got up, bowed once again and left the room.

"The rest of you, except Charlise, leave us."

"Yes Master." The other three murmured and were about to rise when the figure spoke again, "And Devlin, remove this." He sneered.

Charlise looked on as her companion raised her husband's body with his control over Air, and they silently left the room. Another tear landed on her cheek and she surreptitiously dispersed it into minute droplets so that all that was left was a slight tightness over her skin as the salt solidified.

* * * * *
– – – –

A loud knock rang through the chamber and with the figure's call of "Enter." A visible change appeared in his façade. His eyes took on the magical blue color and all signs of the maniacal black disappeared. His features softened as the door opened, and as he stood up, the cowl hiding his face in mysterious shadows, fell back to reveal his visage.

"Your Majesty." The new arrival in the Throne Room bowed. "My Lady." He greeted Charlise, around ninety years his senior. "How may I be of service?"

"Noah, my son." King Rusoe stepped forward placing a hand on Noah's shoulders. "Your absence these last few months has resulted in the acceleration of your training."

"Your Majesty?" Noah spoke, the question clear in his tone.

"In an unfortunate turn of events, Zeke Farsooth met his end in a recent incident." Charlise stiffened where she stood to the side, but the king continued in his nonchalant manner. "His place as the leader of the Guard is now being filled by Lady Charlise. As the Guard always consists of six members, one for combat with each element and the other three particularly trained in physical combat, we are falling short of a member."

"Do you then wish to confer me the honor of being in your Guard, Sire?"

"Yes." The king answered.

Charlise knew that he was hiding his excitement beneath the composed façade when Noah simply raised his chin in submission. "As my king wishes, so it shall be."

'Foolish child.'

"Very good." King Rusoe commented before gesturing to Charlise to pass him the same knife which had slid through her skin earlier. The king repeated the ceremony with Noah, drawing out another single bead of glistening red blood which slid down his exposed throat ever so slowly.

Then, "Kneel, my servant," and Noah knelt. She had to make an effort to keep the scoff that rose within her at his anticipation. Noah had been an intelligent man in her eyes, but now his intellect was failing him as the glory clouded over all doubts that should have arisen at the king's words.

"Kneel to pledge yourself to me, to protect me and to follow my will in all that I command. Kneel, and then rise to glory. Rise to be a part of the Guard, the Ancient Guard which consists of Lady Charlise, Lady Seyliyef, Lords Elmor, Trey and Devlin and now you, Noah Winters. May you bring honor to your stature till you hold the position."

Noah rose as King Rusoe handed the knife back to Lady Charlise and then spoke again, "My son, whenever a new Guard joins in, they have to do an initiation mission, acting as the leader for all the other Guards. This is to test their ability as a member."

"I live to serve, your majesty," Noah's reply was exactly what was expected of him. *'At least some of his wit still remains.'*

"Your mission is to capture Melissa Hayes."

"The runaway?" Noah asked clearly surprised. "Was she not apprehended about a month ago?"

"No, son, she was not. She is here in Peritia, disguised as Myra Mills, the girl we met a while ago, with dear Eleza. Surely you must have seen her change form momentarily? Though I'm quite interested to know why her magic faltered. No matter, it is you duty now to capture her and imprison her while she awaits her long due trial for the murder of Lord Killian and Lady Freya."

Noah nodded his agreement slowly, an action which she could see was not originally intended by him, as he said, "I promise I will do my best, Sire."

'He has to be trained to control what his body reveals.' It was as if Charlise had been filling a mental to-do list. The only way to honor her mate's memory was to keep another from destroying their life too.

"See that you do," King Rusoe said, his tone altering slightly and an almost imperceptible wave of magic washed over the room, which Charlise knew for a fact that Noah would deny later.

"Go, rest now, both of you. You will need your strength for planning and execution."

Lady Charlise and Noah both bowed once again, and with murmurs of 'Good night, Your Majesty's, they departed from the Throne Room.

A slight smile played on the Monarch's lips as Charlise noticed that his irises were once again invaded by intermittent fluctuations of black.

* * * * *

The moment Charlise and Noah left the Throne Room, she flicked her right wrist and a hidden knife slipped into her awaiting palm. It was the same blade which had belonged to her late husband, and had then drawn her, and Noah's, blood. She followed him and in a sudden surge of fury she grabbed Noah's shoulder and pushing him against the wall of the corridor, leveled her knife with his throat. "Kingling, beware. Do not fail this assignment because I just might be the first person to hunt you down."

Noah smirked slightly and acting lightening fast, caught her arm, twisting it behind her back, he turned her so that she stood with her back touching his front. She felt him lower his mouth to her ear and he whispered menacingly, "Do not worry, My Lady, I will not fail. However, if you cross my path, take heed, that in case of the plan's failure, I would be the one hunting you down."

Charlise gasped as he released her, lips raised in a smirk of her own as she watched him saunter down the passage. *'I might not need to do much for him after all.'*

Red

She ran blindly in the dark, chill nipping at her bare feet with every step she took. The path she took apparently going on forever, and closing in on her, the darkness intensifying with each passing second.

Danielle recognized the situation as one of her recurring nightmares, the darkness reminiscent of the time she had been locked in the cellar by her first ever foster sibling all those years ago, where she had cried silent tears until she was let out six hours later. It was then, after seeing how her captor had laughed at her appearance, that she had decided to keep her emotions in check and her expression blank, if she wanted to stay away from home. *'No, from Rebecca and David.'* she had told herself then.

Suddenly, she stopped running, as abruptly as she had started. Elle thought that maybe her magic would help her, even if the situation was just a dream. *'Sun, fire, warmth, light.'* She thought over and over again, as she had for the tests, and slowly but steadily, the blackness around her brightened. However, what she saw in the now illuminated corridor was even more terrifying than the stifling darkness had been, a chill running up her spine in spite of the new warmth.

The walls were a deep, blood red color, the ceiling too low for even a non-claustrophobic like her. The corridor's end was not visible and she could not see the door from where she had been either. The walls pulsed as if they were alive, their surface rippling, forming ghastly faces, most of them silently screaming as if in pain.

Danielle shuddered and sank to the white marble floor, hugging her knees to her chest. She rocked on her heels like a scared little child, her eyes closed, the agony too much to see. She could almost imagine hearing the screams, the moans, the wails, the keens. And then, "Danielle... Sweet Danielle, get up love, you can save us."

She did not recognize the voice, but the tone was enough for her to open her eyes again and with a sudden burst of happiness and peace in her heart, she placed her palms on the right wall, caressing one of the now still faces, for it was that face that had called out to her, the face of a small child. It smiled at the touch. Words popped into her mind then and following her instinct, she spoke them aloud.

"Your work now done it's time to leave

I promised my return, in you I believe

Be free, for you deserve it

And with the light of your wake may the world be lit."

The walls stopped transforming at her touch and words, and as she looked on, the red color of the walls turned into a haze from its earlier solid form, and then disappeared, the now bare white walls of the corridor echoing with the sound of joyous laughter, the trapped souls celebrating their freedom.

* * * * *

Elle woke up with a gasp, disoriented, and the first thing she saw on opening her eyes was the reddish pre-sunrise hue of the sky outside her east-facing window, the color slowly growing and mixing with the indigo of the night sky. The color reminded her of her dream and her grip on Dan's hand tightened.

He woke up almost instantly. "What happened?" he asked, looking around, searching for the cause of her alarm.

Hearing another person speak brought to memory the voice she had heard in the dream, and this time she recognized it, though the realization was quite confusing as well as horrifying.

Confused by her silence, Dan tugged at her hand and asked, "What?"

Elle uttered the last word that she had spoken before falling asleep. "Noah." She said in a loud whisper.

* * * * *

Noah Winters sat up with a gasp in his room in the palace, as memories assaulted him. He felt as if a part of him had been missing for a long time and that it had just returned. He groaned at the new onslaught that his thoughts invoked, remembering with horror all that he had forgotten.

Five years old Noah Faeleth was skipping through the corridors of the palace, his home for as long as he could remember, one hand clasped with the king's.

"Uncle Rusoe? Are we going to the playroom? I wanna go there." He pouted adorably. "I wanna play with Liana and Zephyr. Uncle Rusoe!" he tugged at the elder lamia's hand.

"Silence!" Rusoe snapped. "Shut your mouth and don't ask questions."

Noah paled at this, but complied with the order. The two walked through the palace, taking so many turns that even if he wanted to, Noah could not remember the way. A nagging feeling in the back of his mind told him that that was the purpose.

After about ten minutes of running around on his small feet to keep up with the king's long strides through the corridors, rooms and 'shortcuts' the two finally stopped in front of a plain looking door at the end of a passage.

When Rusoe opened it, Noah tried to pull his hand away, terrified at the dim red light in the corridor into which the door led. Having lost his patience, Rusoe simply picked little Noah up and carried him through the door which shut with an ominous creak. As if powered by Rusoe's arrival, the light in the corridor brightened, the shadowy faces on the wall eliciting a whimper from the scared child.

"Come here boy." The older man barked, pulling Noah to the right. He grabbed the little child's hands against his will, with him still struggling, placed them on the wall. Noah could feel something grab hold of him, and no matter how much he pleaded, cried or pulled, he could not remove his hands.

In the background, Rusoe chanted.

"Anim vestra ligati sint mecum.

Your soul bound to me,

Your powers mine

To do with as I please

Till my wish, or the end of time."

Noah felt pain like never before, as if his very being was tearing apart. With a tortured scream and a tear stained face, he collapsed. The king laughed, finally having made a pawn of the new 'heir'.

* * * * *

Beyond that, all that the new memories consisted of was constant pain and agony, being forced to cede his magic against his will. Noah remembered having his body being Compelled due to the control over his soul, to do things he wished not to. From that period, all he remembered was the excruciating pain he experienced when he tried to make a stand against the exploitation of his powers. He remembered his physical self being separated from his actual identity, his name being changed from Faeleth to Winters, and his mind changed Magically many times whenever he thought of things remotely relating to anything that might have led to the discovery of this bondage. And his anger grew.

The anger suddenly melted away with the arrival of a woman, whose clothing alternated between normal garbs and a robe made up of pure light and magic. He hazily remembered calling out to her, calling her… Danielle? And then her reaching out to caress him, the first touch of love his soul had felt in twenty two years. He remembered the fulfilling joy he had felt when that woman… No. *Luca*. Had spoken and how freeing it had felt when he finally joined his other half.

Suddenly another scene flashed in his mind, that of standing in a corridor that very afternoon, waving at Eleza and her companion, Myra was it? And her momentary transformation which he now recalled clearly, through which she became the same angel that had rescued him. 'Danielle' he had called her. *'But hadn't the king called her Melissa? Oh Lorelei, he ordered me to capture her!'* Noah thought, with a sudden realization.

'The king.' A growl escaped him, unconsciously expressing his utter fury. *'That lying, manipulating, heartless maniac!'*

Thinking back to his captivity of over two decades, Noah saw red and snarled, "I'll kill him."

However, suddenly his savior angel's face rose in front of his mind's eyes along with Rusoe's orders. *'I'll save her, and then I will kill him.'* He decided, getting out of bed, determined to warn her, whoever she actually was, before he had to meet the Guard to plan for her capture.

'Eleza. Eleza knows where she is.' He concluded and left the room, slamming the door behind him, not caring if anybody heard him.

* * * * *

Inside the Royal Chamber in the West Wing of the palace, the king awoke with a sharp pain to his chest. Beside him his wife, Lady Maebel, stirred, "What happened?"

"Nothing. Go back to sleep. I'm going to take a walk." He spoke tonelessly.

Lady Maebel hummed a reply and slipped back into sleep.

King Rusoe climbed out of the bed and moving to his study waved a hand to open the curtains. Nothing happened. He tried filling a glass with water. Nothing again. He gestured to light the torches, with the same result. His eyes widened and with a horrifying realization, he ran out the door. Weaving through hidden passages and shortcuts, he quickly reached a door which had always remained closed except when he opened it. It lay wide open. He entered it and saw exactly what he had suspected with a sinking heart. Bare, white walls. He let out a frustrated scream and then leaving the room, sprinted to a nearby hidden door which led to a small room, almost a broom cupboard. There, sat a very old lady who looked to be around eighty years outwardly, which meant that she was actually around two thousand six hundred years old in reality.

She raised her head when he barged through, and taking one look at his expression and wild, now non-flickering, common brown eyes, Lorelei broke into a still-full toothed grin, and said, "So the prophecy comes to pass at last."

Compromise

Eleza jolted awake when she heard incessant knocking on her door. She flicked her gaze to the window as she was getting out of bed and groaned when she saw that the sun had not even kissed the horizon with its first rays yet.

"Coming!" she called out, forming a plan to punish her visitor for waking her up at that ungodly hour. Eleza snatched her robe from a hook behind the door, quickly donning it as another fusillade of raps rang through the door. She got ready to drowse whoever had disturbed her sleep, water which was earlier in the glass beside her bed now collecting above the door frame, on standby and opened the door.

Being drenched in cold water was not something that her visitor appreciated. Dispersing the offending substance with a flick of his wrist he growled, "Stop messing around El."

"Noah? What are you doing here? Weren't we supposed to meet tom-"

Noah cut in, "I need to talk to Danielle."

A moment of shock later Eleza rambled, "Danielle? I don't know any Danielle. Do you mean Dan? I mean Daniel Hayes? I last saw him yesterday morning when he came for training, I haven't seen him since."

Noah rolled his eyes and put his hand on Eleza's still moving mouth to silence her. "You know that that's not who I meant, although I might have a chat with him about you one of these days."

She shook her head against her 'brother's' palm and was trying to remove it when he continued. "I am asking you about the girl Danielle, the one who is disguised as Myra Mills, your companion last afternoon. Do I need to specify any further? I am not asking, I am ordering you as a member of the Guard to comply with my demands and answer me."

Forgetting her shock for a moment, Eleza's eyes widened because of another reason altogether than the earlier one and she hugged him. "A member of the Guard? Already? That's amazing! Congratulations!"

Noah pried her hands off him and offering her a sad smile, said, "It isn't all that it's hyped up to be. Now come on and take me to her. This is important and I don't want people noticing me leave."

She was confused by his dull response towards a job which he had harped on about ever since he had known of it, and also his apparent need for secrecy regarding Danielle. Eleza regarded him for a moment and then nodding towards the corridor outside, said, "Alright, I'll follow your command and take you to her, but not because of your stature, but because you were already supposed to know. Now stay quiet and follow me."

Noah rolled his eyes at her words and saying, "When have you ever known me to be loud? Worry about yourself you clumsy kid," followed her out.

She playfully threw back a glare at him as they walked out of the residential wing towards the gardens, wherein lay a hidden exit between the trees. An exit that they had built more than a decade ago. It was coded to them through blood magic, an extremely dangerous and foolish task at the ages of fifteen and ten, but extremely effective and strong too. And so, it was through this exit that they left the sleeping palace behind and moving as quietly as they could, made their way towards the Hayes Mansion, albeit unknowingly, in Noah's case.

* * * * *

After trying to wring out the prophecy from Lorelei using methods he had not before, a very short list that was, unfortunately, with the same result as all the times he had tried before, nothing.

Not even a word. Just a smug smile, on the face covered with a light sheen of sweat, eyes glinting with pain and also knowledge that was oh-so-valuable, known to none but her. He left her, as unsatisfied and frustrated as he always felt after visiting her.

Not paying attention to the fact that it was not even barely day yet, he roused a servant and bid him to ask Lady Charlise to report to him in the Throne Room as soon as possible. Then, with a quick detour to his study, King Rusoe strode purposefully towards the Throne Room himself, in wait for his Guard to present herself.

* * * * *

"Charlise." The king said, his non-magical brown eyes, hidden behind ordinary blue contact lenses, trained on her figure as she knelt by his feet.

"Yes Master?" she could not quite hide her wonder at his summons so early in the day.

"You have been my faithful servant for ninety years now, and for that, I thank you."

"The honor is all mine, Master." She spoke as was expected of her, even though she deeply wished that she could simply take out her late husband's knife and stab his murderer straight through the heart once and for all. However, she knew that if she even tried to, he would kill her with a mere flick of his hand. And so, she compensated with just a slight clench of her fists by her side.

Unaware of his Guard's thoughts, the king continued, "Since Noah is handling... the other task, I hope that you would assist me in one of the rather important situations that has arisen."

"I'll do everything in my power to follow your will, Master." She answered, internally rolling her eyes, wondering what fool's errand he would give her to further undermine the new 'leader' of the Guard, bitterly remembering Zeke's death that had led to her acquiring the position.

"Follow me." King Rusoe spoke silkily, the slightest his of hysterical frustration and anticipation leaking into his tone, something which Charlise, in all her wisdom and experience, failed to note due to her inner monologue.

* * * * *

Charlise wondered at her Master's intentions as he led her through a maze of passages stopping in front of a door that somehow emanated evil and she had an inexplicable urge to run away from that unassuming door. "Come see my life's work." Rusoe gestured as he opened the door and stepped in, the lights lighting up as his walked further in. She brushed aside her nerves by laying her hand on the hilt of the knife hidden in the folds of her robe, holding on to it for courage just like her husband had when it was in his possession. And then she walked gingerly into what appeared to be a long, very long, corridor, with white walls, marble floor and a low ceiling.

"Master, I do not quite understand. What is this place?" she turned to face him, suddenly terrified at the almost hungry expression his face.

He smiled. "I told you. It's my life's work."

King Rusoe's smiles unnerved her and she unconsciously withdrew the black blade, holding it in front of her, as if ready to attack.

The king's smile widened and acting too fast for all her training to deal with, he unarmed her and pushed her to the wall, pressing her palms to it. Charlise gasped at the pulling sensation that she felt, as if her very life, her soul, was being pulled out of her. She threw a panicked gaze at Rusoe who looked positively un-human as he spoke the words which he had last spoken twenty two years ago in that very same place.

"Anim..."

* * * * *

He watched as her features grew old. Wrinkles appearing, the skin becoming translucent and loose with apparent age and her hair turning rapidly white as her very life force was sucked out of her slowly and painfully. She tried once more to pull her withered hand away from the wall, but before she could do so, she collapsed, her hands un-attaching themselves as her figure crumbled.

"I had no choice." the words rang in that corridor of torture as the king stepped over the corpse. With a smile playing on his lips at the sight of the now pinkish hue of the wall, he left the room without a second glance, closing the door with a wave of his hand, an unnatural wind helping him.

Light

The colors red, orange and pink blossomed at the horizon, slowly spreading towards the inky blackness of the night's sky, hinting at the inevitable sunrise and the last stars of the night dimmed and winked out of sight as they became the first lights of the day. The soft light barely illuminated the woods, very little light actually filtering through the thick canopy. Two figures moved quickly through the trees, using the slowly fading darkness to their advantage by keeping to the shadows. They were very near the paved road when the larger of the two figures staggered.

"Noah!" the smaller figure cried out, the voice decidedly female. She caught him just before he fell, and leant him against a tree trunk for support. He steadied himself and the gingerly got up.

"You alright?" she held out a hand, ready to help if needed.

"Yes Eleza, but we need to hurry. Something's wrong."

Her eyes grew wide in the semi-darkness and she simply clasped his arm, tugging him on as they continued to make their way to what they hoped were answers, though their progress was slower than before.

* * * * *

Dan and Elle had moved to the kitchen, where he brewed a cup of chamomile tea to soothe her, while she sat on one of the high chairs beside the island, tracing random patterns on the granite counter-top. Dan had asked what she had seen in her dream that left her so shaken, but Elle found that the more she tried to remember it, the hazier the details became. She felt the now-familiar tingle in her chest, which indicated magic at work and panicking, she called out- "Dan-!"

Invisible hands choking her cut off anything else that she might have said, and she clutched at her throat as the cup slipped from Dan's hand to shatter on the marble floor when he heard her and rushed over.

Spots appeared around her vision and Elle managed to get out, "Corridor...Red...Souls-", before she lost consciousness. Her last thought was, *'Who was the figure in white near the sink?'*

Dan caught her, just as she crumbled to the floor, and with his shouts for help ringing through the house, he carried Elle in his arms to the nearest room, which turned out to be the living room, where he laid her down carefully on the couch.

* * * * *

When Elle came to, she felt a cold weight resting on her forehead. She knew that she was lying down, and that someone was tracing circles on the back of her right hand.

"-Don't know what happened. She was sitting, but then she called my name. I turned and she looked pale, just... so pale. And then she collapsed. She said something but I couldn't understand it. I'm sorry Gramma, I'm so sorry." Dan was speaking softly, and he choked on his next words. "For a moment there had been no pulse. She was cold, and all my fire wasn't enough..." Elle felt Dan turn her hand and lift it up to his cheek, which was scratchy from a slight stubble. "So...cold."

Her eyes fluttered open as she caressed his face. "It's okay Dan, I'm okay." She whispered, her voice hoarse from the earlier assault.

"Oh thank Lorelei!" Anlynne spoke from where she was sitting near Elle's head. She removed the wet cloth from Elle's forehead, her frown and the disarrayed state of her appearance displaying her worry.

Elle sat up after Anlynne had checked her eyes for signs of a concussion (and declared in the negative) and gave the older witch a nod of thanks. Then, for the first time ever, Elle pulled Dan to her, hugged him and placed a small kiss on his temple. "I'm here."

They sat like that for a few suspended moments, Elle bending down from the couch and Dan leaning up from where he sat cross-legged on the carpet. Squeezing slightly the hand he still held to his cheek, Dan pulled back slowly and then giving her a tired smile, he got up and walked over to the center table. Anlynne sat down beside Elle then and they watched as he picked something up. Elle noticed that he tugged his shirt's sleeve down to cover his fingers and picked whatever was there with that pseudo-gloved hand.

He held out a small sealed envelope saying, "This came for you after you…fainted."

She reached to take it from him and he pulled back, "Careful!"

Elle snapped her head up to look at him questioningly. "It's hexed." He said simply, and held up his other hand whose fingers were red enough to make someone believe that they had been recently stung, and healed. "I got off easy as I dropped it as soon as I touched it, but there's something sinister about it."

Anlynne offered her insight on the topic. "The Revealing charms showed that there is some kind of detection charm placed on it which checks the unique magical energy of the person touching it. These kinds usually have dire consequences for those who are not meant to touch it. Dan got off easily, though Soleus knows that I've told him enough times not to go near anything whose source you do not know." She glared at Dan at this and he ducked his head in embarrassment.

She nodded but still reached towards it. The three of them let out a collective sigh of relief when Elle's first contact with the envelope resulted in no reaction. Anlynne and Dan watched as she gingerly ran her finger across her name scrawled on top of the pristine white paper, and turning it around, similarly traced the seal.

She felt the tingle of magic, and just like while meditating, she prodded the blue wax gently with her mind. Elle could barely control her gasp when she felt the actual amount of magic contained in the seal for the first time. Further mental probing led to her hearing the softest of whispers which echoed in the confines of her mind. *Danielle Hayes... only for Danielle Hayes. Just her... nobody else... Burn the others, drown them. Pull the nails of their filthy fingers off one by one... hurt them...hurt all of them. Irreparably.* Horrified, she tried to cut off the connection but felt as if she were trapped and could not escape from the snares of the seal's magic. She struggled against the magic as it continued to list out horrible ways in which it would treat anyone who was not her. Abruptly, the magic seemed to sense her identity and the whispers grew louder, *Danielle Hayes... yes you are Danielle Hayes. Danielle Hayes, open me!* The last couple of words were almost a shout in her mind and she finally managed to snap out of her mental prison, her breathing at a quick but inconspicuous pace.

'Don't let them know. Don't let them know.' One of her first defensive tactics ran on a loop in her now safe mind, and Elle proceeded as if she had not been moments away from what could have been a fatal hex, had the magic not recognized her.

Daniel and Anlynne had no idea of the mentally exhausting ordeal and they watched in silence as Elle carefully broke the seal and took out the folded paper from within it. It was a small message and Elle quickly went through it, though anger for the unwarranted hex rose in her with every line that she read. It really was not that dangerous a knowledge that would justify what the hex was meant to do to someone who was not the addressee.

She clumsily got up and walking over to one of the lit torches nearby, dropped the envelope along with its content in it. The fire blazed with a sudden red glow and then returned to normal.

"Anlynne, would you mind if I talk to Dan alone?" Elle said, an unblinking stare fixed at the greedy fire which had devoured the letter, her back to her family. A sound from Anlynne indicated that she very much did mind it, but then seeing the tension and determination in Danielle's statue like form, she made her retreat. "Call me if you need anything." She said as she left, but her tone clearly expressed her displeasure at having been evicted so unceremoniously and it was evident to the siblings that she would not, in fact, come if they needed anything that day.

Elle's anger steadily grew as she stared into the fire, the destroyed words running on repeat in her mind.

Elle,

Don't speak. Don't try to think about it. Let go of the dream for now. It's bound by someone far greater than you can imagine. Let. It. Go.

-Melissa.

* * * * *

The moment the sound of Anlynne's steps stopped, Elle rounded up on Dan.

"Who was she?"

Dan looked perplexed at her words. "Who?"

"The woman in white who dropped the letter off." She spat harshly, her self-control on the verge of disappearing entirely as the hex's intentions along with what it could have done to

Dan along with the even more confusing contents of the note sang like sirens to her rage.

"What?"

"You heard me." She snarled. "Who. Was. She?"

Dan put out the fire, which had appeared on the couch due to her emotions going haywire, with a glance. He held up his hands, and spoke in a calm and controlled voice that further aggravated her. "Elle, I have no idea what you're talking about."

Elle was going to interrupt, but Dan ploughed on. "There were just the two of us in the kitchen when you fainted and the letter arrived. No one else."

"So close." Elle groaned as she sank to her knees on the carpet, exhausted mentally and magically.

Dan walked over and knelt beside her. "What happened?"

"What happened is that someone choked me to prevent me from speaking about my dream and then the hexed letter from mum told me the same thing essentially. Even now," she made a choking sound. "Even now I'm not able to speak anything about it." She wiped away a stray tear which had made its appearance after her frustration and exhaustion.

"The woman in white?" Dan prodded, bringing Elle back on track.

"I saw someone. She was standing by the sink. I felt her coming! Just like with the other letters! It was her. She dropped it off."

"Elle, I didn't see anyone."

She gave him a look. "You were facing the other way. How could you have seen her?"

Dan raised an eyebrow mockingly, "And you were about to burn the house down earlier because…?"

Elle swatted at his arm and glared. "I was angry. At her. At me. We missed the chance Dan."

He rubbed where she had hit him. "But now that you know how it feels when she comes, maybe we'll have better luck next time?"

"Maybe…" Elle was still doubtful.

Dan helped her up, but before he could say anything else, three loud knocks echoed through the house. They caught each other's eye and Elle then looked over to the grandfather's clock standing in the corner. "Who could it be at…five in the morning?"

"Don't know… come on, let's check. Lynni's upset anyways, she won't come down. We'll have to go and apologize later though."

* * * * *

Noah and Eleza slowly trudged up to the imposing gates that led to Hayes manor. He still felt inexplicably weak, as if part of him was numb. The Hayes' trust in them showed when the extensive safety wards placed around the property let them pass even at such an early hour.

He thanked his Guard training for not being much startled when a voice floated over to him.

"Noah."

A flick of his wrists created a fireball in his left hand and a small dagger slipped into his right palm. In a fraction of a second his whole demeanor changed into that of a warrior, all signs of fatigue gone.

"What?" Eleza hissed, looking around, every bit as alert as he was, though unarmed.

A laugh echoed over to him, making him clench the handle of the knife and the fire blazed hotter.

"Where are you? Show yourself!" He whipped towards the source of the laugh.

"What are you talking about? There's nobody here!" Eleza looked at him with scared eyes.

She had not seen him like this in months. He had told her that the Voices had ceased and she had believed him, but looking at his wild expression she was not so sure anymore.

"Calm down, Kingling." This elicited a mixed response from Noah. The words themselves invoked a thrill of fear, reminding him of Charlise's threat, but the voice... the voice was *Luca's*. That voice... That voice would never hurt him. And the fireball extinguished.

Noah slid his dagger back into its holster and relaxed his stance. He still kept on his guard though, but he was sure that no harm would come to him while his *Luca* was there.

"Will you tell me what that was?"

"It was nothing."

"Fine." Eleza snapped and walked on.

"Noah." The voice spoke again, from his left. He was not someone who usually believed in the preternatural, but after the night he had had, he would have gone along with anything.

Especially something spoken by his *Luca's* voice. He nodded slightly to show that he was listening.

"Don't talk to Danielle about the corridor. She isn't ready for the knowledge. You'll know when she will be, but till then, don't talk to her about it," The whisper carried over to him as he felt someone take hold of his hand.

Noah was startled for a moment, the frown on his brow hidden by the slowly dissipating darkness. Then he intertwined his fingers with the invisible ones of his *Luca* walking beside him. The softness and the warmth of the small hand in his confirmed that she was not a figment of his imagination, but something quite tangible instead.

Although the slight crinkling at the corner of his eyes hinted at an almost smile, her words confused him.

He was about to murmur a question to her when he realized that they had neared the main doors and that Eleza was lifting up the griffin head to knock.

Noah's hold on his *Luca*'s hand tightened infinitesimally as the sound rang through the house. Eleza looked back at him, totally unaware of their invisible companion, he saw her eyes softening a bit as she took hold of his right hand, and squeezed gently as an apology for snapping. Noah blinked in acknowledgement and then looked back to the door as the latch inside it clicked to open.

He could not help the smirk that rose at the sight of a surprised looking Daniel before his gaze slipped to the figure half hidden behind him. *'Myra'.*

He only had a moment as their eyes met, for he felt an acute pain in his chest and could manage only an "Oh." as he lost consciousness and the world went black.

* * * * *

End of Book One

For those who cannot wait, here's a little something of what's waiting for you in the next book…

Knowing Me

Prologue

He almost grinned as the knife slit his victim's throat, the third one in five days. *'I'm getting slow.'* He thought as the warm fluid gushed out, and he could almost feel the soul seeping out. As he muttered the familiar words of a Binding spell, his thoughts torn between disgust and glee, he thought, *'Lamias.'* Even the way that he thought the word made it seem like a curse. *'Stupid, stupid Lamias. Give an ape some magic and they forget how to defend themselves without it.'*

He sighed as a burst of energy surged through him, water this time. This was getting annoying. Harvesting souls had been actually fun the last time he had been on the Hunt. So many deliciously powerful souls, trapped for his use, with no one being the wiser. Oh how beautiful the Hunt used to be! Poisoning a family with an untraceable venom and after the Harvest, leaving them in their beds, as if they were peacefully asleep, except for the grey pallor of their skin, the only explanation that the others gave to justify the deaths was that the victims died of shock. And this gave rise to the belief that something unnatural was abound. It was the thrill of being a secret, of being the object of nightmares that excited him. For he was all that, but none were sure of his existence. Well, people had known of him, 'Faet' they called him, a deadly mix of the supernatural and the Inevitable. However, the powerful, the ones who could have stopped him, *'Or tried to!'* he sniggered, were ignorant of him, lost in their world of finery and polite hatred.

He wiped the blood off the blade of the knife with his fingers, bringing them up to look at the dark liquid in the silvery moonlight which filtered through the canopy. Then, cleaning his fingers on the dead man's clothes, he flicked his wrist to set his victim's body on fire, simultaneously controlling the air so that no smoke might be seen. As he watched the corpse disintegrate into ash, he thought back to his rise to power. It had been so easy to find sympathizers, ones who helped him Harvest, albeit unknowingly. They thought themselves to be clever thieves, stealing from the poor, killing them was simply collateral damage. After all how could they let the victims go if they attacked them in retaliation? He gave a hollow laugh as he remembered the night he had killed them. *'Faet, indeed.'*

'And look at me now, down to killing with knives once again.' He scowled in the darkness, knowing that he could not overindulge in the Hunt and Harvest. *'Shame the Gates are closed. How easy it would have been to simply go over and demand submission.'* Then he was gone, slithering through the darkness like the Devil he was, ash being the only thing which was a proof of him ever being there, the blood long since Vanished.

And then an unnatural breeze blew the grey and white specks away.

* * * * *

See you in the next book!

-DV

About the Author

Divyanjali Verma is a short-story author, novelist, and a poet. She started her first book at the age of sixteen and is currently working on the second book of her series, Intempus. When relaxing, she can be found reading while listening to music, or watching movies. You can also read her other works at fromabusymind.wordpress.com.

Printed in the United States
By Bookmasters